WINNIPEG
WITHDRAWN
D1204456

Massacre River

Massacre River

René Philoctète

Translated, with a note, by Linda Coverdale
With a preface by Edwidge Danticat
and an introduction by Lyonel Trouillot

A NEW DIRECTIONS BOOK

Originally published in Haiti as *Le Peuple des Terres Mêlées*
Published by arrangement with Alain Philoctète

Manufactured in the United States of America
New Directions Books are printed on acid-free paper.
First published clothbound in 2005
Published simultaneously in Canada by Penguin Books Canada Ltd.
Design by Erik Rieselbach

Library of Congress Cataloging-in-Publication Data
Philoctète, René.
[Peuple des terres mêlées. English]
Massacre river / René Philoctète ; translated, with a note, by Linda Coverdale ; with a preface by Edwidge Danticat ; and an introduction by Lyonel Trouillot.
p. cm.
ISBN 0-8112-1585-7 (alk. paper)
1. Dominican-Haitian Conflict, 1937—Fiction. 2. Haitians—Dominican Republic—Fiction. 3. Dominican Republic—Fiction. I. Coverdale, Linda. II. Title.
PQ3949.2.P53P4813 2005
841'.914—dc22

2005015034

New Directions Books are published for James Laughlin
by New Directions Publishing Corporation
80 Eighth Avenue, New York 10011

Table of Contents

Preface

Between Haiti and the Dominican Republic flows a river filled with ghosts. This river is called, aptly enough, the Massacre River and is one of several natural frontiers, dividing what is geographically one island into two independent nations.

The Massacre River claims its name from a seventeenth-century battle between French and Spanish colonizers who were fighting for possession of the island. Along the lush banks of these then vigorous waters, the Frenchmen and Spaniards butchered one another to the point that the riverbed seemed crimson with blood. Over time, the river has lived up to its designation and has been the site of several other brutal massacres — including the one that is the subject of this tour-de-force novel by René Philoctète.

In March 1995, when I decided to visit the Massacre River as part of my research for my own novel on the 1937 slaughter, all of this was on my mind. So when I got there, I expected to see a river running with blood. In the shadow of such a gruesome history, I told myself, how could there be anything else?

On the Haitian side, where I went to meet the river, is Ouanaminthe, a small border town with just a few thatched and wooden houses dotting the main roads. (Now it is the site of a so-called free-trade zone and has been invaded by slums, underpaid workers, and labor-laws abusers.) However, at that time Ouanaminthe was a much more agricultural town than Dajabón, the adjacent Dominican town, whose ice cream parlors, open squares, and large government edifices could be spotted from the edge of the Massacre River.

When I got to the river itself, I found that it was simply a tiny braid of water running beneath a concrete bridge and into the distant plains. The sand in the riverbed was dark brown and close to the surface of the water, which was slow-moving, almost stagnant. Where was the high current forced to engulf hundreds and hundreds of corpses in 1937?, I wondered. The torrent towards which poor Haitians fled when, as Philoctète put it, death seemed so tangible that it had set up shop everywhere. However, what this extraordinary novel reminds us is that sandwiched between the two borders was a group of people who tried to build a new world, people who were as fluid as the waters themselves, the people of the Massacre River. Without realizing it, it was those people I was looking for, people like Philoctète's memorable characters, especially Pedro and Adèle, who suffer, but also sing in the pages of this book.

During that visit to the Massacre River, I found myself meeting many of the living people of the river. There was the woman who sat with two small basins of clothes in front of her as both her feet swayed back in forth in the water. There was also the man who held the rope halter as his mule lapped up the water. Downstream, two poor boys — one Haitian, one Dominican — were taking their afternoon bath, scrunching up their faces each time one spilled a cupped hand full of water on top of the other's head. On the bridge were Dominican soldiers in camouflage uniforms with rifles on their shoulders. Every once in a while, one of the soldiers would lower his head and peek down at the water to make sure nothing unusual was taking place. These were all the new people of the Massacre River, people who though haunted by a gory history still live, sometimes peacefully and sometimes uneasily, side by side.

Having read René Philoctète's *Massacre River*, I grieved then, as I do now, for all the Massacre River's survivors, those who suffered the machetes that chopped the Haitian heads and the fingers that counted the dead. However, my hope was renewed by the spiritual children of the river, the washing woman, the man with the mule, the bathing boys, the soldiers, even the characters of this book, who not only inspired the love and outrage of an extraordinary writer like Philoctète, but continue to challenge the meaning of community and humanity in all of us.

– Edwidge Danticat

René Philoctète: A Dream of the Triumph of Goodness

We might begin by saying that René Philoctète was born in Jérémie, Haiti, in the Département de la Grande Anse, one of the last verdant corners in a country where nature has been ravaged by the hand of man and the hazards of geography. This by way of explaining the strong sense of place which radiates throughout Philoctète's writing. When asked about his work, he sometimes replied simply that there was a tree that he loved along the Route de la Grande Anse.

We might begin in a different fashion by noting that the literary oeuvre of René Philoctète comprises ten collections of poems, four plays, three novels, and a book of short stories. The published work, that is. Because no complete inventory yet exists of the manuscripts he entrusted to various friends and family members. We might point out that in the early 1960s, Philoctète was one of the founding members of the group Haiti Littéraire, along with Anthony Phelps, Roland Morisseau, Serge Legagneur, Davertige, and Auguste Ténor; that Philoctète was also, a few years later, one of the co-founders of the Spiraliste literary movement with Jean-Claude Fignolé, Frankétienne, and Bérard Cénatus; and that both these movements marked a resolutely modernist departure from the traditional esthetics of Haitian fiction and poetry. René Philoctète was an integral part of every artistic adventure in his homeland from the early 1960s to the late 1980s: cultural centers, literary clubs, writers' associations, and so on. We might also mention his long career in education, his devoted service in the "difficult profession of teaching," and his generous support of Haitian youth, to whom he gave unsparingly of his time and encouragement in spite of his fragile health (he suffered from high blood pressure and diabetes). We might well pay homage to his considerable influence on the Haitian writers of today.

Furthermore, we might observe that from his birth on November 16, 1932, to his death on July 17, 1995, René Philoctète left his native land only twice: in 1966, when he fled to Quebec along with many intellectuals, leftist militants, and simple citizens driven from Haiti by the horrors of dictatorship, and in 1992, when he accepted a literary award from the Argentine parliament.

Although he arrived on a one-way ticket, Philoctète's exile in Canada did not last long. At that time, the "good doctor" François Duvalier was tossing students, poets, and trade unionists into the dungeons of Fort Dimanche. Two founding members of Haiti Littéraire had already paid dearly for their talent and political convictions: Anthony Phelps spent some time in Duvalier's prisons, while Auguste Ténor never emerged from his cell, adding his name to the endless list of those who vanished without a trace. And so, in 1966 Philoctète joined the Haitian exodus and followed his friends to Montreal, but he remained abroad for only six months. Home again, he asked "that my country open her welcoming arms to me upon my return," and with Frankétienne, Jean-Claude Fignolé, and a few others, he would symbolize — for those of his compatriots still living in Haiti, and able to read — the vital language of hope. A "hands-on" poet, he was a man of tireless goodwill and boundless enthusiasm, always busy, his desk and study a monument to literary clutter. How many writers of my generation came to poetry beneath the back-yard mango tree of Ti René! "Li'l René" 's door was always open, no matter the hour, the weather, the political climate, or the state of his finances.

More than a gesture of bravado (and there is no cowardice in fleeing the prospect of imminent death), his return to Haiti was an esthetic choice, as if the poetic act could be born only on the ancestral soil of the Caribbean isle of Ayiti Boyo Kiskeya. By coming back home, he sought to safeguard his writing from despair, and in *Ces îles qui marchent,* a collection of poems written upon his return, he wrote: "My comrades [in Montreal] play the games of rueful children. They invent in December a bright sky on which they draw a hang-dog sun to lead around on a leash like a do-nothing king."

René Philoctète's second trip abroad lasted a few days, long enough to accept the sole literary honor he ever received outside of Haiti. For although his return to Haiti was essential to his writing, his audience was limited, because his entire literary oeuvre was first published in Haiti at his own expense, in a few dozen copies that were poorly printed or even simply mimeographed on cheap paper. Ti René was not an expert seducer bent on insinuating himself into the ranks of the powerful in a quest for fame. He shared his poetry with a few friends and with the young people he welcomed into his home. He knew nothing about the promotional strategies, the wheeling and dealing that foster great careers. And in those days, suffering from a form of racism or condescension, the international press and the university scholars in the West chose to believe that Haiti was populated exclusively by victims and executioners, by paupers and thuggish Tontons-Macoutes. In the eyes of the West, under the reign of Papa Doc, the best of Haiti was to be sought elsewhere.

We might ponder the workings of chance or prejudice that govern fame and reputation. This writer, almost unknown to non-Haitian "specialists" in Haitian literature, is without a doubt the most *present* in the literary memory of Haiti's current generation, the man who upheld the language of confidence in the country in which no one has any confidence anymore. The man who called its myths back to life, took up the burden of its history, and told its story. The man who spoke the language of the Haitian people's dignity while urging them to join the other peoples of the Caribbean in a common destiny. The education that molded us insisted, through its lousy history lessons, that we were shoddy goods — because of our race, or our origins, or our poor excuse for a culture. Above all, this education taught us that we could not be both fully Haitian and completely modern. Philoctète has been our guiding spirit, championing his culture and all cultures, his Haitianness and every form of humanism: "Will I be fortunate enough to finish my long journey by bringing the voice of my country into full-throated harmony with other worlds, even to the pitch of love? Love that springs into being . . . ." Philoctète is the man for whom Haiti's ordeals did not betoken a lack of humanity, but obstacles to be overcome, like all life's problems. To his Haitian readers, Philoctète was the man who, through words, faced the worst and dared to dream of the triumph of goodness. And of beauty, too. "Taking the side of beauty, [Philoctète's poetry] remains essential to us. No lightning rod can shield us from the thunder of his voice," writes the poet Georges Castera.

We might point out, finally, what is tender and disturbing in the writing of René Philoctète. Resolutely eclectic in its composition, happily pillaging any means to its end, his work constantly asks the age-old questions of literature: how to conjure form and meaning, wordplay and reflections on life; how to assume one's modernity while grounding oneself in a sense of real history and place; how to speak of the immediate and the timeless, of here and everywhere. Philoctète's work opens (and sometimes precedes) the current debates animating conferences on the literature of the Antilles and the Caribbean. His style is generous, assertive, demanding, and its intention is clear: to speak with a Haitian voice to the hearts of all humanity.

The last time I saw René Philoctète, a few weeks before his death, he told me, "I was born during the [first] American occupation of Haiti and I will die under a new occupation." His voice, cracked and weary toward the end, was always raised against misfortune, always seeking, in everyday life and in dreams of the future, the goodness of the world.

– *Lyonel Trouillot*

Massacre River

Monte Cristi
Puerto Plata
Terrier Rouge
Ouanaminthe
Dajabón
Gonaïves
Mont Organisé
Santiago
San Francisco de Macoris
Saint-Michel
de l'Atalaye
Cerca Cabajal
La Vega
Sanchez
Samaná
Hinche
Saint-Marc
Thomassique
Cotui
Sabana de la Mar
Elías Piña
Las Matas
Lascahobas
El Seibo
Sabana Del Cuey
Port-au-Prince
Los Llanos
Higuey
San José de Ocoa
Jimaní
Azua
San Pedro de Macoris
Duverger
La Romana
Petit Goâve
Baní
Santo Domingo
Pedernales
HAITI
DOMINICAN REPUBLIC

—1—

Since five o'clock in the morning, a bird — to be honest, no one knows what it is — has been wheeling in the sky over Elías Piña, a small Dominican town near the Haitian border.

The children think it's the kite the local boss sometimes flies to kill time. The adolescents would love to straddle it for a joyride. The adults don't seem worried about it, but deep down, they're hoping the thingamajig will go away. Jaws jutting, eyelids blinking, the old folks slide sidelong glances at one another, spit three times on their chests, and cross themselves.

Suddenly, the bird hangs motionless, wings spread. Its shadow carves a cross that cuts Elías Piña into quarters. No sound leaves its throat. Not one twitter or chirp. The bird is mute. Dogs, cats, oxen, goats, donkeys, horses bite, claw, graze, browse its shadow set in the crystal of a Caribbean noon.

Señor Pérez Agustín de Cortoba, the boss, the government representative, is dozing, ensconced in a wicker armchair on his freshly whitewashed veranda, while a half-dozen flies buzz about on his beige potbelly, bulging out from beneath a black sports shirt. In his siesta, he dreams of Emmanuela, his *negrita* who left more than a week ago for Cerca-La-Source, in Haiti. He clenches his fists: he strangles the unfaithful woman. The only distinct word among those disgorging from his gullet: "*¡Muerte!*"

Between a hiccup and a head-wobble, he opens a bloodshot right eye. The eye swivels toward the bird, smiles, closes. While the fingers squeeze . . . until the nails scrape his palms raw.

Meanwhile the bird takes life easy in the village sky. An elderly hunter armed with buckshot peppers it with a hail of pellets that rebound in an arc to the ground, squashed flat.

There is no blood in the bird.

Swallowing his spittle once, twice, thrice, the old hunter goes home, his head hanging. A loud report rattles the neighborhood. The old hunter has just blown his brains out.

No one attacks the machine with impunity. Pablo Ramírez tried once; he was thrown into the quagmires of Lake Enriquillo. The caymans ate him. Sonia del Sol and her four children (Miguel, Sunilda, Mario, Marco) hanged themselves in Barahona. Roberto Sánchez disappeared. Now his voice no longer lullabies the nights of Santiago de los Caballeros.

"Neighbor, do you know the story of Paco Moya? They say he was a sailor, in the capital between voyages, and died under suspicious circumstances, a starfish between his eyes."

"*¡Verdad!*"

"And the story of María, *la puta*? Of José, *el poeta*? Of

Rafaelo, the baker? Of Juan, *el campesino*? Of García, the teacher? Of Enrico, the tailor?"

"Death lowered the drawbridge, the castle swallowed them up."

No, no one attacks the thing. Or else children waste away and women piss blood between their thighs.

The bird is a sorcerer.

With one fell swoop it plummets, head down, onto the trees. Leaves go flying, branches break, flowers catch fire. The impact against the trunks does not stem its fury. Everything collapses in its wake, leaving it free to maneuver.

The bird is blind.

Now it shoots skyward, wings folded, feet together, drilling the air. Struck head-on, the sun quivers, shrinks, caves in. No one dares to comment on the missile's acrobatics or even *try* to cast a counter-spell.

"Neighbor! Tell us the story of the arrow with which the Cacique Caonabo took Fort La Nativité."[1]

"The stone has returned to the sky."

"And in what season does the Yaqui flash its fires in La Vega?"[2]

"The fires are dying of their own brightness."

"Tell us the song the Caribs sang before going down the paths of war."

"That song has flown away."

"Neighbor! The warriors' flame still dances in our eyes!"

Numbered endnotes can be found beginning on page 221.

"No, that was the time of men, and that time has passed."

"Like overripe fruit that rotted on the vine?"

"Yes. Like overripe fruit that rotted on the vine!"

Only Roberto Pedrino, a vacationing sociology student visiting his cousin Antonia Felicia Salvador y López, tries to appease the creature's anger, by playing the mandolin. But his fingers on the instrument's strings shrivel up to their roots. Undaunted, with his teeth Roberto César Pedrino plucks chords from the instrument — any chords at all! — that tangle, squeak, whistle, flounder. And playing back-up to the notes of Roberto César Pedrino y Márquez, the corrugated-metal roofs of the houses begin to screech, cackle, cheep, and mew. The emboldened inhabitants of Elías Piña take up whatever comes to hand — drum, flute, saxophone — and troop through the streets to music that murmurs and neighs. The bells in the wooden chapel of Notre-Dame de la Conception quit their tower, calling and jostling one another with the rapid-fire sound of weddings.

How long does that last? Nobody in Elías Piña can say. Except that at six in the evening they are still parading around to the din of cymbals, the squealing of guitars, the thunder of drums, the moaning of saxophones, and the hysteria of the bells.

Enveloped in his ample black cassock and assisted by two peevish, toothless, verminous, and hunchbacked old women, José Ramírez, the Andalusian priest, even drenches the crowd with streams of water consecrated pronto to that purpose in the name of the Trinity and poured into big saffron-yellow earthenware basins.

No one wonders why José Ramírez Pepito y Biembo threw hundreds of bars of soap into the holy water. And strangely shaped, rainbow-hued bubbles slip hissing from everyone's mouths: green ones with gargoyle heads; pink ones rippling like parasols; crudely grimacing black ones; bubbles as white as sails, yellow as autumn, blue as the high seas, red as the fires of rose gardens and the waning moments of engagement balls. (A kind of fugue from the village orchestra.)

Meanwhile, after hounding the sun into a corner, the device reappears in the sky over Elías Piña. It buries its head under its left wing and sleeps, suspended between the fields and the first stars.

The beast is deaf.

No one knows where it comes from.

"Hey! Hey! Señor Pérez Agustín! Is this thing from around here?"

Of course! Don Pérez's red eye tumbles down his beige belly, disturbing five or six flies along the way, and stops at the huge navel to say "*¡Claro!*" Climbs back up, pops back into its socket. In the meantime his fingers, finishing their throttling of Emmanuela, fumble to caress her.

"Come, now!"

We are its guests, just possibly its children. Anoint! Anoint thy nation and thy bride, thy people and thy lamb! The old hunter tried to shoot thee down and brought about his own death. Carlos Fuentes rose against thee; the Sierra de Bahoruco smothered him. Angel Toya threatened thee; he rotted away in Macorís. The thing watches over us. So who fears it? It's a Dominican affair. *Una cabeza de la tierra. ¡La primera cabeza de la tierra! ¡La cabeza nuestra!** Let us kindle a blaze to warm its vigil. Saint, saint, saint, thrice-blessed Rafael Leónidas Trujillo y Molina![3]

And Don Agustín congratulates his eye.

On a binge, the bells peal out their arpeggios. Without any prompting, children gather dead branches and fragrant leaves. Men toss into the air lighted matches that fall in a luminous necklace onto firewood transformed into a mass of sparks, madly changing colors like chameleons, trembling, writhing, burning the night of Elías Piña. Women cut off their hair — cascading black braids gleaming like deep water, loose tresses smooth as corn silk — and toss it into the flames. Whirls of blue, green, pink smoke swirl away the charred odors of violets, chamomile, and basil, sowing them across the plowed land, strewing them beneath the stars. All while the thing broods a nightmare above Elías Piña.

On his candy-pink porch facing Don Pérez Agustín de Cortoba's veranda, the alcalde Preguntas Feliz, the number-two man in the village — light brown skin, a thin figure in clinging rust-red trousers, right hand holding aloft a late-eighteenth-century wrought-iron lantern, left hand over his heart — begins to sing a kind of slow merengue.[4] Like an Adoration. His slippery voice paralyzes all others, vanishes in the distance and returns; spirit of the times, it seeps into

---

* A homeland head. The first head in the land! Our head!

everyone and everything (the springhead shivers; the butcher's dog curls up in a ball; the daughter of Don Miguel, the surveyor, has one of her fits), going deep, settling in. As on a throne. "By the eyes of the Madonna and the gold of the sierra, we hail thee, Lord of blood and horror!" shouts the alcalde Preguntas Feliz. "Lord of the dreadful blood!" bleat the villagers. A child starts sniveling after biting his tongue. With a menacing finger, Preguntas Feliz shows him the late-eighteenth-century lantern. The child chokes back his tears. The man of justice, left hand over his heart, holding the lantern out toward the villagers, fine-tunes his Adoration: "By the power of the agony we hail thee, Lord of demented death!"

Pérez Agustín de Cortoba, befogged until that moment in his noon siesta (and the flesh of Emmanuela), stretches, hiccups, reopens the red eye. Hiccups. Wipes away the thick drool on his beige belly with a hairy left hand. Stretches. Farts. Stands up, waves his arms around, sways from side to side on his crooked bowed legs, and to the tune of "The Blue Danube" sings: "For the head of a Haitian man, the accolade of Trujillo; for the body of a Haitian child, male or female, the smile of Trujillo; for a Haitian woman hacked in two, the gratitude of Rafael Leónidas Trujillo y Molina!" Hiccups.

The villagers try to take up Don Agustín's song, but their voices seem stuck. Are they appalled? Just plain ashamed? Or afraid?

Slipping furtively along, Preguntas Feliz, slim as a stiletto, steps down from the candy-pink porch into the street and slices through the crowd. The lantern swings gently from his hand as he heads — chin up, eyes front — toward Don Agustín de Cortoba. Who, shambling heavily, leaves his whitewashed veranda to fall into the street (crushing people) and the arms of Preguntas. They huddle together in the center of the prostrate, frozen village. Their voices, one thin, the other booming, clump together, merging for the paroxysm of the Adoration: "The reign of the dagger is within heart's reach, announcing to the loyalty of the people the coming harvest of death." Their faces in the dirt, the villagers mumble: "Thou whose firmness hast taken precedence over our plans, thou who hast anointed us with the oil of obedience, mayest thou be truly welcome. O thou! Here, there, and everywhere, lord and master of the alliance, may the wine of solemn allegiance be served to thee!"

Elías Piña recites the glory of Trujillo. Recites until night stops up every throat and each mouth gapes mutely.

So it goes while the contraption, hovering between the fields and the stars, continues to brood a nightmare, and piled-up machetes lie resting, recuperating for the next onslaught on Haitian heads. The bells are quiet now.

Carefully bound and gagged, silence stands guard over Elías Piña.

Pedro Alvarez Brito, *el mulato dominicano,* a worker at the sugar factory in San Pedro de Macorís, who had neither sung nor wept nor spoken nor even looked at the bird-lord, the raptor-kite, the sign-bird, touches the right hand of his wife, Adèle Benjamin, *la chiquita negrita haitiana* from Belladère.

And finds it freezing!

"Adèle!" says Pedro Brito tenderly.

"The day of blood is coming closer," murmurs the young woman.

"Yes, the signs are everywhere, they're obvious."

"The day of shame and scorn . . ."

"Is it possible?"

"What isn't possible when power turns stupid?" exclaims Adèle in exasperation.

"Don't forget our common humanity, sweetheart!"

"Our only protection, *hombre!*"

"We should be able to manage."

"No doubt through love, Pedro?" asks Adèle dreamily.

"That's right, Douce Folie, my Sweet Madness."

"But love is crippled, *hombre!*" cries the young woman.

—2—

More than a hundred kilometers through the scent of cut grass. It's such a long walk to the factory! And it takes so much sweat! Adèle did not sleep last night. My body did not absorb her warmth. Her eyes did not shine in the comfort of the bedroom. Adèle inhaled the odor of slaughter. Her veins ran cold.

"You're still awake, Adèle?"

"The time for dreaming is over."

Gorged on light, the bee feels sluggish when night falls.

"And our crop of yucca?"

"Don't count on it too much. Life sleeps with death."

Death has never seemed more tangible. It has set up shop in our life, it's like an advertisement. Everyone fawns over it.

"Didn't you hear the church bells? They're stirring up fresh blood, Pedro."

As if plowing his body, the smell of cut grass invades Pedro Brito. He coughs. Disturbed at its dawn bath, a turtledove cleaves the air with a slate-pink light.

"Did anyone really hear the bells, Adèle?"

"*Sí, hombre,* the bells of the death agony."

And yet, the roosters sang for a long time in the darkness.

That happens when they have stuffed themselves with too much corn: stoked with the stolen fires of heaven, the golden grains set the roosters on fire. This time, the birds had a bellyful of too many nights, and their crowing has scattered the gloom.

"My love! How pure the dawn is in its jeweled finery!"

"Yes — dawn and our kisses when our lips crush together."

When the press squeezes the cane, the juice lights up the sugar-factory boiler with a thousand solar flares. It took us some time to understand the transparency of our lives. Now that the curtain is coming down, we acknowledge the splendor of this fairy play, and that's how it is whenever we lose something. Each time a kiss comes to an end, we become aware of its lingering taste and honey. Man is a creature of nostalgia.

With an angry hand Pedro Brito decapitates a pale flower whose name he does not know. A bitter perfume clings to his fingers. He dips his hand in the dew. The scent stays bitter and strong. Like the presence of the beast, or the servants of savagery. Don Pérez Agustín met the lieutenant two nights ago, not far from my home. Without a word, the lieutenant simply handed a sealed letter to Don Agustín, who remained silent as well. Adèle had sensed what the orders were. Her hands were shaking.

"Pedrito, do you think it's almost time?"

"There is more than just death, *loca!* First, there are death's errand-boys."

"No doubt."

"And they're even worse."

Pedro shreds the pale yellow flower with his fingers. They turn red. The thing has laid eggs among the flowers. It has lain with the high road. It has stalked through our dreams. It has taught the sky to scream. It sleeps in the cradles of our children. It slips between our sheets. It sits at the head of our tables. It formulates our plans, molds our habits, conditions our reflexes, controls our feelings, develops our ideas. It shapes our lives. Pedro Alvarez Brito spits his curse into the grass. A *Mimosa pudica* folds up. We measure ourselves against the horror of the beast: we begin to resemble it. Praising its authority, our children draw its profile on their slates. People say the thing will be part of us until, losing ourselves, we find ourselves completely changed. Paws, hoofs, claws instead of our conscience and our hearts. The wingspan and shadow of the thing in lieu of pity, and peace.

Pedro quickens his pace. The plain stretches away into a green distance dazzled from time to time by a scarlet flight of ortolans. Frightened, dawn has sought refuge beneath the pinions of birds. The madness will not be unleashed today, of course, but everything is ready. The sealed orders leave no room for doubt. Don Agustín de Cortoba, crammed into his khaki uniform, has seen Don Preguntas Feliz. They have smiled. They have embraced. A fine coupling of cunning and atrocity: Preguntas, the man of laws and subtleties; Agustín, the man of arms and blind anger. The lieutenant was not talkative. Authority in action has no need of words. Harangues, allocutions, proclamations, philippics — these are for elections. And the people rush to the polls. When you elect death, there is no need to vote. Preguntas has pronounced it legal. The lantern has shown what time it is. Trujillo has made his decision. Don Agustín has placed his fat hairy hand on the alcalde's right shoulder. The two of them have had coffee. Have made faces. Perhaps their coffee was . . . ? That's why Adèle was shaking when she watched me uneasily enter the dawn.

"Will you come back, Pedrito?"

"Who can stop me, *mujer?*"

"The beast, of course! Racing across the plains, scaling the mountains, flying over the seas, striding over the towns, that beast is a herald! It has proclaimed the order of the day."

When the cane fields burn, stalks twisting in the flames become so many lighted candles, inviting admiration of the disaster, fostering the acceptance of cruelty. All autocracy has its magic, its seduction: the troops on parade, the bright flags, the thunder of marching feet. And the people, enraptured, approve, forgetting that those who tried to dispel the darkness have been swallowed up in the solitude of dungeons. Miguel Salvador came to grief, with a thin blue line distinctly visible around his neck. Somola *la negra,* the musician of La Romana, was raped in the prisons of Monte Cristi; her black body with a wide hand tattooed in white on her belly was thrown to Colonel Ramón Del Sol's dogs. No one has yet discovered what happened to Enrico and César Gonzalez, the two sons of Salomón Gonzalez, a baker in La Loma. When trumpets blare, when banners wave and martial steps resound on the paving stones, the people, glutted, applaud. Comforted by the courtesy of the populace, authority unsheathes its claws and dares to give orders like a bloodthirsty ogre.

"But we'll see each other again, Adèle, my love. And I will protect you."

Striding through the dew just beginning to burn off, Pedro Brito brushes by a tuft of basil. The air sneezes, somersaults, breaks its nose, all in a daze. Bewildered insects jiggle their mirrors of spinning colors: from saffron yellow to pure violet, from jet black to the pellucid white of waterfalls. Beautiful, beautiful, beautiful, these lands! Both of them together. One high, the other low, with their underground sortileges: the Zemis' gold,[5] the sweat of those wrenched from Africa. The Cacique Caonabo knew Anacaona,[6] the *samba*. The tenderness of Jaragua was dissolved into the pride of the Cibao Valley. Flowers discovered the intoxication of bravery. When the hurricane blows, the teals whirl in circles — a fragile crown in the vigor of the gale.

Pedro Brito crosses a stream in which glitter the last jewels of the sky. In a few hours I will meet with *los compañeros*. Machetes will cut the cane; the sticky juice will cling to the stalks. The muscles of two peoples will work together to bring forth the goodness of the Dominican earth. Ah! The smell of the canebrakes on a clear morning! As if the earth wished to bless the sky. Pedro Brito flares his nostrils greedily, inhaling the life of the island in whiffs of warm air. The land here bears my footsteps, which can surely be heard on the other side. In the other land, my land! The caciquess visited the cacique, and their fires burned brightly for a long time, from coast to coast. Adèle understood perfectly when she said: "Is it possible to separate us when I have become flesh of your flesh?"

Pedro hurries a little faster. Dawn has been shipwrecked, strewing noble debris: rims of clouds, corroded stars, mists lost on the violet flanks of foothills. A frank and royal early-morning sky spans the two lands, the low one here, the high one over there, strangely serene!

Pedro stops walking. Tumbling over the cane fields, the peasants' voices rush to his senses, catch in his throat. He breathes with delight both this direct presence of the earth and this fraternal warmth of honest toil coming to him from beyond the plantations. The sky sets the trees of the Sierra de Neiba aflame, and the breeze arrives to rustle them in a silent shimmering of deep-red gems sifting down through the branches. The Sierra becomes like a clear glowing fire where every wing drinks deeply, every roof gathers radiance, every water hole takes nourishment. Standing tall, gazing toward the light, Pedro watches the Haitian earth turn rosy in the distance, astonished that the land should be so lovely, wondering at his birth in such a marvel, for both lands are marvelous. Amazed, he sets out again, trailing after him the breath of his country. His step is light. He feels this. Feels reassured. Adèle will not go to Boc Banic, across the border. Pablo Nuñez may well have sent home his wife Antonine, who is from Belladère, but Adèle, *la mujer mía,* will stay here.

She is this heat coursing through my body, this laughter throbbing in my blood. If one of us went away, the other would languish and die.

"I've never imagined myself without you, Pedro. Not even once."

"Neither have I — the song never soars without the voice, Adèle."

"Nor will the nightingale trill without the branch."

"Or else there would be no cradles, or havens."

"And yet, paths and roads are closing down like eyelids."

"Yes, Adèle, if you see things only from the outside."

"But you know, Pedro, I have in my body all of life, and the voice of ecstasy as well."

Let Celio Márquez send his wife Sanite off to Maribaroux, in Haitian territory — me, I am keeping Adèle at home in Elías Piña, on Dominican soil. And Señora Victoria, whose husband, Monnuma Saint-Hilaire, crossed the border near Capotille last night! How she's suffering, *la viejita!* With six children on her hands . . . Every evening she runs out in the moonlight, hoping to pick up the trail of her man. When she's had her fill of the night, she goes to sleep at the side of the road, a bruised smile on her lips, her fingers in the dew, her heart drifting among the stars. Poor old woman, she'll die of longing! Alberto Rava refused to allow Marcelle to leave home for Ouanaminthe, in Haiti. A home is a seed planted in the earth. It must be whole to grow, to bear fruit. Cut in pieces, the seed rots. Marcelle already has a big belly, like a plump melon. Soon the house will brighten with a new smile. "No, Marcelle will not be going to Ouanaminthe," insists Alberto Rava. I share his way of seeing things. Adèle is the sweat of my labor, my holiday, my resting place, my afternoon stroll. She is what makes the morning bright, the night sweet. She is my fear, my daring, the path that crosses mine. And what road could I take if she fled from me?

"Ah! One false step, and everything is lost!"

"No, Adèle. I've placed landmarks along the way. To guide us."

"Don't ever think that I want to give up."

"Not on your life! You're not a gloomy person, but you've talked too much tonight. Sleep, now, it's late."

"I'm not as depressed as Juan always claims."

"Juan is a doctor, he must know. For the moment, if you cannot be right, at least be wise, and sleep, kitten."

"You sound like a reverend old priest."

"A pompous professor, that's me. Now, sleep."

I keep her with me the way the peel keeps the fruit. It's delicious to feel the whole fruit between your teeth, rind and pulp all in a jumble. Even Emmanuelle, the concubine of Don Agustín de Cortoba, the government's chief representative, has fled Dominican territory.

Freed from the snare of the Sierra de Neiba, the sun gallops across the two lands. We'll have to join forces to defend them. We people from here and over there — we are, in the end, the people of a single land: Joseph Eliassaint from Léogâne, where Anacaona reigned, the queen with the face of a Zemi;

Pierre Jean-Charles, betrothed to the daughter of Orlando Sapini, a carpenter in El Paso; Antoine Jean-Félix, who cut cane in Macorís and now lives in Anses-à-Pitre; Josué Pérard, born in Petit-Goâve, whose father, Aristide Pérard, lies in the cemetery in Capotillo. We have to regroup, close ranks, and talk to one another, understand one another so that Mass may be said for a single people, bread may be blessed for the same mouths, and the same hearts may have a chance at the good fortune of love. We'll gather up our two peoples for grazing rights, for blessings, for sharing, for putting our heads together, for hands-on action. This land supports us, and we must defend it. I can already hear the machetes in the cane fields. O my love! If the monster dies, I promise you...

In the sky, the bird goes round in circles. The song of the canebrakes chokes off. The sun becomes muddled. A vast cross carves up the fields. The oxen, donkeys, dogs, cats graze, bite, browse, claw the image of the contraption. The oxen, donkeys, dogs, and cats chew on shadow, then gaze at one another, stricken, their eyes flooded with immense tenderness.

—3—

At the very end of his infancy, Rafael Leónidas Trujillo y Molina was in love with that tremendous-thing-near-the-sky called the Citadel.[7] Kites with mermaid tails, steel hoops scraping the asphalt with their tongues of fire, colorful balloons over the roofs of Santo Domingo, marbles, little boats flitting around ornamental ponds, plush animals, toy figures, spinning tops — nothing enchanted Rafaelito Leónidas Trujillo y Molina. He wanted only the Citadel. Unable to get his hands on it, he lamented his fate morning, noon, and night. But cherished the hope that one day it would be his.

The Citadel became ever more deeply rooted in his memory.

The thing is, before Rafaelito was even ten years old he was already gorging himself on the stories told on the street corners of Santo Domingo by grannies in their black mantillas. The pace and vividness of their narration usually determined the child's judgment of the characters and events depicted.

So hearken to granny:

"They came from the West, passing through forests, over lakes and mountains, past perfumes and birds, and on a night of Caribbean heat, the soldiers of Toussaint Louverture[8] poured into Santo Domingo. They slaughtered the livestock, thrashed fruit from the trees, diverted rivers and streams, stopped the clocks."

The granny paused in the story of the soldiers from the West, relighted her cigarette butt, and after a quick puff, returned to her tale.

"Louverture's soldiers stayed with us here in the East for a long time. They grew gardens, laid out roads, built houses, married our daughters, had many children to whom they taught the language of the land and the trees."

The granny got up, shook the dust from her skirt and, lost in the clouds of her cigarette, hobbled off into a nearby alley.

The audience, after some hesitation, melted away. But Rafaelito stayed there, as if the legend of Toussaint Louverture were continuing all by itself... or as if his *chiquito dominicano* noodle might at any moment, then and there, grasp the profound meaning of the story.

Suddenly, he scampered home, dashed into his room, rummaged through a cupboard, and pulled out a newspaper in which he read straightaway: "The Haitian cities of Lascahobas, Saint Raphaël, Hinche, and Saint-Michel de l'Attalaye must return to the Dominican Republic." He burst out laughing, apparently with satisfaction. He mused aloud that instead of the "language of the land" the granny had mentioned, he would have said: "The covenant of blood."

He examined his conscience. And that day, he took himself seriously.

Citing the Treaty of Aranjuez signed by France and Spain in 1777, the Dominican political vanguard repeatedly laid claim to Haitian territory along the border.

Courses in schools and universities exalted dreams of conquest and the spirit of Dominican nationalism. Musical groups composed works around this theme. Religion evangelized in the same vein. It was the only topic of conversation. The media kept everyone focused on this single goal.

Meanwhile, such a mood led to almost chronic unrest along the border between the Republic of Haiti and the Dominican Republic.

For the young Trujillo, Haiti became, a priori, an adversary. And the Citadel, his phantasm.

—4—

Pedro Brito is thinking of his wife. He begins to shiver. What if the *compañeros* don't listen to me? "Alfredo Pérez! Listen. Sergio Moreno!" *Dice* Pedro Brito that the hour of the massacre draws nigh. We already know what's brewing. The sign is in the sky over towns, villages, military posts and outposts. "Hey! *Amigos.* Antonio López! Félix Labur! Alfonso Vargas!" Ah! The sound of machetes stifles my voice. Filthy factory — it has long chewed up our flesh, and now it's swallowing our voices. "Molina Díaz! Miguel Sabrino! Hey! Pepe Sánchez!" The way things are going, they've probably had the beast shoved down their throats, too. "*¡Amigos! ¡Compañeros!* Guillermo Sánchez! Juan Passito!"

The water in the stream clings to Pedro Brito's legs. He runs his hand over it . . . and finds it red with cockroaches. Pedro starts to run. So do the cockroaches. The sky, birds, children, women, old folks, the Sierra de Neiba, the Yaqui, grasses, smells, Queen Anacaona, her Zemi face, the Virgin of Higüey, Puerto Plata, Alcalde Preguntas Feliz, Padre Ramírez, the Guardia, Don Agustín de Cortoba, the bells, Lake Enriquillo, the two Lands, flowers, the dawn, the sun — all slip into Pedro Brito's hair, pawing him, sizing him up, in a horrible game of blindman's buff! Then the grasses, the

Virgin of Higüey, Alcalde Preguntas Feliz, the women, the Sierra de Neiba, its sorcery, the old folks, the Yaqui, Don Agustín de Cortoba, his whitewashed house, the flowers, Puerto Plata, the two Lands, the dawn, Padre Ramírez, the Guardia, Queen Anacaona, her Zemi face, the smells, Lake Enriquillo, the sky, the bells, the children, the birds, the sun . . . stop, dissolve, disappear in a pervasive but flabby silence.

A green lizard on a white rock swallows the last of a black butterfly whose wings seem hemmed with gold. Pedro lets out a wild cry. Blood is coursing down the trunks of trees, as a warm, gentle breeze ruffles the leaves in their crowns. The butterfly has split open the lizard's flank. A wildcat with glowing russet fur streaks away through a clump of mint. The air grows giddy. Fluttering stickily, gilt-edged black, the butterfly alights on a dwarf rosebush in flower. A clot forms a knot in Pedro's throat. He spits. A red fountain gushes from the broken mint. Even inside me! Is it really the mobilization of Death? And for what? What hatred? What venture? What shame? What punishment?

Along the road, not far from the sugar works where Pedro Brito is heading, rumbles the engine of an olive-drab truck packed with armed soldiers: a hair-raising sight . . . Passing his hand over his face, Pedro finds it moist with perspiration. Farther away, in the four winds of the sky, a voice tosses off a bolero:

Sunrise is blinding me with its light
The morning dew could not soothe me
I'm going away on the path of night
With no shadow to keep me company.

High overhead tumbles an ocher cloud. Everything is there for the glory of Trujillo. Adèle is right. No! It's a savage transmutation: everyone is in the village square: workers, professionals, civil authorities, soldiers, nuns, executives, children, parents, servants. Massive, total, direct participation. Unconditional acceptance of an agenda of ideas, a state of affairs. Of mind. The mikes crackle. Everyone huddles under the same carapace. Concurs with the sharp-fanged words. Abundance becomes scarcity. Liberty buys itself chains. Brotherhood strikes a deal with genocide. Mutual congratulations. General embracing. Pats on the back for everyone. We're all in the same boat. And we'll run like rats, if the ship sinks. There's no difference among us. You lie down with a wolf as with a lamb. The lamb howls? The wolf bleats? We huddle together under either skin. Indifferently! Perfectly at ease! One's no better than the other. We become a mass. We gorge ourselves on platitudes. From speeches to applause, we complete and perfect ourselves. Shedding our skin. Collectively! Me, Pedro Brito, I refuse to join in. Everything must become normal, human. We must put an end to the nightmare. No one attacks Monsieur le Président with impunity, I know. Miel Roca perished at San Pedro de Macorís. Orlando Díaz was shot down in Samaná. Maybe I'll wind up in a hole in La Romana. But we must stop the machine in its tracks. Our comrades will understand this. Adèle believes this, in spite of her fear. *¿Por qué tiene miedo?* Why are you afraid?

Both peoples will help to foil this plot . . .

—5—

To obtain the Citadel, the child Trujillo was prepared to do anything. Trade the mortal remains of Christopher Columbus. Divert the Ozama River. Demolish the Convent of La Regina. Clip the wings of the birds in La Vega. At times he felt himself the master of the fortress or believed that he carried it upon his person, like a lucky charm. He did not allow anyone to approach him, for fear they would steal it from him.

As he grew older, the child Trujillo became increasingly eccentric.

Things were no different in the seats of power in the Dominican Republic. People were absurd. They wrote on the white walls of municipal buildings all across the country, in big, black, block letters: "*¡El diablo haitiano!*" They partook of the Eucharist while cursing the men of the West. They organized public meetings at which they distributed tracts against their western neighbors. Along with machetes and the Dominican flag. In military barracks, reveille was sounded at intervals, day and night, to keep the troops on their toes. Firing ranges were set up on marketplaces. Men went through the motions of hand-to-hand fighting, the parry-and-thrust of fencing, combats between athletes, fighting cocks, boxers. Everyone devised tactics. Explained strategies. Invoked the spirits of their ancestors.

People went on with their ordinary lives, but felt on the verge of chaos. No violence had as yet led to violence, but everybody spoke freely of violence. In the shadows, imaginations were rising like bread dough.

Despite this public panic, two heads of state, Haitian and Dominican, met at Thomazeau "with a view," they proclaimed, "to strengthening the bonds of friendship" (as the phrase goes) "between the two countries," which (incidentally) only the accidents and interests of colonization had cleft in twain.

One evening during that same period, during a reception at the town hall of Santiago de Los Caballeros, a young Haitian woman was led in. Pressed to sing a song, she chose a lullaby from her native region:

If the hand does not feed the mouth,
What will happen to the hand?

The adolescent Trujillo was present at the fiesta in the town hall of Santiago de Los Caballeros. After listening to the lullaby, he admitted to his uncle, a soldier in the Dominican Army, that he hadn't understood a word.

–6–

At last Pedro arrives at the sugar factory closest to Elías Piña. The pistons hiss, throwing off jets of boiling oil. Soot gets into every last little corner.

The men are surprised to see Pedro, and a few even seem dismayed. Pedro thinks immediately of his wife: "Is it her death, already showing in my face?" The workers become more and more upset; some draw back, while others appear stunned, and now Pedro is afraid: "Will I really be able to save Adèle from the massacre?" The workers show such revulsion and behave so bizarrely that Pedro finally explodes.

"Why are you so scared of me?" he shouts angrily over the din of the machinery.

"Have you slept with blood?" shoots back an old carrot-colored man perched on a wooden stool.

"You got fear written all over you!" bellows a guy almost lost in a cloud of steam.

"Not a pretty sight!" brays a bare-chested young mulatto with only one arm.

"For God's sake!" growls a black man clothed in brown, who appears on second thought to keep the rest of his opinion to himself.

Pedro feels utterly desolate. It's as if the whole world were mocking him, taunting him, insulting him, hurling stones at him. The workers were his only hope, his sole support. And now they're . . .

"Pedro Brito! Pedro Alvarez Brito y Molina! What's happened to you? I hear you're frightening people!"

Pedro recognizes the voice of Guillermo Sánchez. The clear, frank voice of Guillermo. More powerful than the shrieking of the motors.

"I saw the soldiers, *compañero* Guillermo. Perhaps there's still a trace of them in my eyes," replies Pedro.

Now the Dominican workers are truly alarmed. Realizing the situation has worsened, they sense that blood will really flow. One man worries about a Haitian friend; another remembers his Haitian godfather; yet another is in despair over a Haitian cousin. A husband already weeps for his Haitian wife.

"You did well to come," says Pablo.

"It's our cause as well," says Ramírez.

Pedro takes heart, convinced that a deep human fervor can unite the people of the low land with those of the high land, just as the poetic *areitos* of the Golden Flower, the woman of the West, were carried in the quiver of the Cacique of the Cibao, the man of the East.

The clatter of the turbines gives rhythm to the movements of the men in overalls. In Brito's eyes, dawn touches its vines with light. From every throat rise the notes of a merengue, blending with the smell of the crushed cane.

Pedro distinctly hears Guillermo Sánchez, the union boss, in his cream-colored smock all spotted with grease, say to him: "We'll go see the Organization."

—7—

A few kilometers away, however, the bird wheels round and round over the fields of Elías Piña, where Adèle Benjamin spreads out in the sunshine the clothes of her husband, Pedro Alvarez Brito, born, as she was, among the warm-hearted people of the border.

–8–

Water lathers in an aluminum basin. Adèle's quick hands rub her husband's coarse blue overalls, which give off the smell of work, a smell the young woman inhales with sensual pleasure. Along comes an olive-drab truck loaded with soldiers that pauses — just for a moment — in front of Pedro Brito's house, then reconsiders, and drives off with a harsh, low roar. Adéle frowns. She thought she heard the soldiers shouting "*¡Perejil!* Parsley! Perish! Per!" Nonsense! Those are words for people in kitchens or barracks. Adèle rinses Pedro's blue overalls in the basin of clear water. The work-smell makes her sneeze. The truck is parked before the house of Preguntas, the alcalde as slim as a stiletto. What are those soldiers up to, snickering like that? Adèle rises and goes to the fence around the front yard, to glance up and down the street. Everything seems normal. Ordinary. Children are amusing themselves throwing dust in one another's eyes, like those grownups who try to blind others to the truth. "Now *this* year, my dear, I intend to spend the winter in Tokyo. Perhaps in Baden-Baden. In the Fiji Islands. Or else in Abitibi. It all depends." "Well, you see, darling, I plan to join my husband, who is off hunting pumas in the Andes." Oh, sure! Adèle smiles. Yes, it comes to the same thing! The children will grow into adults, of course, and they are presently engaged in the apprenticeship of cruelty. It's perfectly natural. When I was in school in Hinche, the teacher never stopped talking about the carefree world of children, their magical, marvelous universe. But me, Adèle, the *negrita* with the in-your-face hair-curlers, I always thought those wheedling little wonders would soon wander into perversity. Just as a precaution, wait until those first few hairs start growing here and there! Hair is the harbinger of lucidity, maturity. Barbarity. Hair-raising barbarity. What an analogy! Yes, it comes to the same thing.

Now here's Padre Ramírez passing by. He's really dragging his feet, *el padrecito*. Just like Christ at the sixth station of the Cross. Yes. All he needs is the whip. That's it! The whip and the bloodthirsty mob. Come on, padre, buck up! *¡Un poquito de corazón!* The bitter gall, too. Adèle smiles to herself. (*Las espinas también*. And the thorns.) Then wonders why the street is so empty. Not even Chicha Calma, the crazy *guagua** of the border: she routinely hauls her junkyard carcass through the village, hood ornament to the wind, sniffing around everywhere, bothering everybody. Ah, Chicha! How well she knows our tricks, our bright spots, our tumbles, our

* Chicha Calma means "Dead Calm." Chicha is a *guagua*, the Dominican equivalent of a Haitian *tap-tap*, a garishly painted "taxi-bus" (usually a modified truck or van) named after the tapping sounds it emits while laboring up and down endless hills.

rebounds! She has mixed up our colors, and lighted our dark corners. She carries us with all our faults, triumphs, impulses, and secret schemes. Ah, Chicha Calma and her drunk of a driver!

... Nope. Not a single busybody in sight. You mean to tell me all those ladies have gone off to the market in Thomassique? Or Bayaha? You can't be serious! Although ...

I haven't seen even old Josefina, *la viejita* who usually crouches in the shadow of the chapel from dawn to dusk, shouting to all and sundry that she's with child by Señor Anastasio Candido Nuñez y Jiménez, the big landowner. Which that most illustrious person, red as a beet, does not find funny. Where has the madwoman gone? "Hey, neighbor! Have you seen Josefina, *la mulata loca?*" The neighbor lady's dog howls. Its cry joins the dust stirred up in the street by a dank breeze. The blacksmith hasn't opened his doors today. He must have one of those wicked hangovers. The butcher, Rosita Rochas, hasn't opened up shop, either. Now, she doesn't drink, but she must have tossed and turned all night, alone in her sheets and her desires, a widow these past two years! Her husband, by the way, Don Antonio Cabrera, had his throat cut in the prison of Monte Cristi. He was taken to task for not attesting to Trujillo's love of humanity during a political rally in Barahona. "Popular sovereignty is a dogma," he used to preach. "One must believe in it first. And respect it afterward." "Hey, neighbor!" The dog moans in the dust. Or the grocer, either. The olive-drab truck parked in front of Preguntas's house drives off. Or the pharmacist, either. Soldiers stick their heads out, yelling *"¡Perejil!"* This time, I heard it clearly. *"¡Perejil!* Parsley! Perish!" Phooey! Barracks boys or . . . Or the notary, either. Adèle shudders slightly. "Hey, neighbor! Tell me, *dime por favor,* have you seen Josefina? She was carrying a caramel-colored kitten in her arms, a present from Don Anastasio to kill the rats of the full moon. *Dime por favor,* you haven't seen her? Who entertained all comers with the song of the woman wronged? *¡Dime por favor!"* The dog collapses into the dust. Well, looky here! He's crossing the street again, the good Padre Ramírez, lost in his cassock. Christ at the eighth station! Pontius, Pontius, Pontius Pilate, do your hands hurt? Really, *padrecito!* The children play at being carefree. Or malicious. It's incredible! Throwing dust in one another's eyes. Huh! Acting like adults. They'll grow up too, they'll deceive one another left and right. And be corrupted. Hollow men always seek to fill that void with their childhood. In the end, it's only trompe-l'oeil, a leap backwards into a fake paradise, because what is a child? Human ferocity in embryo. A breeding-ground. We chase after images from our childhood and all the time we're our own decoys. Lured into waiting. Hoping. Poor us and our little traps: childhood; the stormy signs of the coming debacle; old age; the chilling realization . . . The doctor hasn't opened his door, either. "Hey, neighbor! Where have our people gone?" The dog is dying in the dust. In the sky soars the bird, imperturbable, hieratic, mute. Adèle frowns. The soldiers shouted: *"¡Perejil!"* What's going on? You can hear the olive-drab truck grumbling off in the distance and snatches of voices hammering out "*¡Perejil!*" The agronomist, either. He must be in Capotille. Where they're slitting the throats of a few pigs penalized for the tax evasions of their owners. What can it cost to declare your porkers? Snouts, trotters, entrails, the whole works. Kit and caboodle! Let's say the liver, 0.10 gourdes; heart, 1.15 gourdes; lungs, 2.20 gourdes!* "Hey, neighbor!" The dog dies in the dust. Pig's guts, that's all! From its split-open belly burst columns of bluebottles that buzz around the street and disappear, humming, into the mouths of the children, who are still throwing dust into one another's eyes. You can't hear the olive-drab truck anymore. It has vanished over the horizon.

Leaving the fence, Adèle goes back to sit by the basin where she left her husband's overalls soaking in clean water. Her husband, gone since dawn. Gone into the dawn. The smell of work rising from the overalls deliciously disturbs Adèle. For two years now I've been sleeping with my man. Every evening my legs have trembled beneath the convulsive jolts of his hips. My whole body has relaxed like elastic in ineffable delights. My eyes have rolled back into climates unknown. I've slid down banks of clouds. Hurtled up through voids, scaled peaks of colors. I've lived in conch shells, abandoned myself to the furor of the lower depths. I've grazed on stars, chewed on words that don't exist. Beneath umbrellas of a thousand nuances and the most varied forms, I have

* One gourde is worth 100 centimes, and five gourdes make a *dollar haïtien*.

been enraptured, my ecstasy endlessly misted by a green and mint-perfumed rain. What worlds have turned before me, been born in me: clusters of lamps gliding past me, the tremulous songs of crystal birds, seas without end melting into rainbows. Oh! This voyage in my body! And when Pedro's lips crush mine, his mouth waters with the juice of my body. And he drinks deeply, greedily, quenching his thirst, while my entrails draw up the nourishing flow that swells my throbbing breasts almost to bursting, so turbulent is the rush of blood to those flushed fruits, and so fierce, so hungry for other sensations, other fevers, pleasures, transports, pangs, and secret places. For two years, despite the gauzy insects that sting my eyes, the aroused music of my voice, the strange veil that hides the ceiling, despite the endless flood of fleecy whiteness and the constant ringing of little bells — when Pedro lies with all his weight upon my chest, navel, groin — despite the welcoming passion in my thighs and the bleating in my throat . . . my smooth, flat, black belly, my twenty-year-old belly with its wine-red beauty mark, has never been able to keep his seed, to declare and show and produce its love. Ah, the breasts! All my man's virile strength has flowered in my breasts. And there alone. My blushing, barren breasts.

Adèle presses her hands against her firm young belly, presses until it hurts, hoping for a quickening, a quivering, a tiny corner of life. Like the stammering of a star. You who are so tender, so gentle when my man enters you . . . but so shy, so selfish it pains me to carry you, my womb!

Somewhere a cow lows, milk spurts. A car coughs in the distance. The engine almost belches up the road. The car squeals. Falls silent. Adèle shivers. *¡Perejil!* What were those soldiers muttering about, as if they'd caught their tongues between their teeth? Never mind — they're . . . Adèle stands briskly shaking the blue overalls. Clear water sprinkles her face. The work-smell intoxicates her. How he slaves away, my old man, *mi viejo!* And what does it get him? Just enough to put one peso aside every two weeks. Laborers, the managers of work and life, are really pawns moved around a chessboard by the bosses in a game that's rigged in advance. But they're hardheaded, workers. No taste at all for murk and stink. Their determination is as rough-hewn as their callused hands, their tenacity as severe as their lean bodies, their humanity as full as their workday. And since they have been sculpted by life, they have the serene weight of the patient progress of history. My man, that worker, hopes today to strike a mighty blow against this inhumanity bearing down on us. He and the others, the sugar-factory men — Guillermo Sánchez, union representative; Sergio Goya, political officer; and Julio César, shop steward — must come to an understanding on ways to thwart the onrushing shadows. "*¡No, compañeros!*" "*¡Si, compañeros!*" "This we'll do, that we won't." "We have plenty of willing hands. But how many guns?" Workers are men of few words. They decide with their hearts, and words from the heart, in emergencies when life is at stake, are understood from heart to heart. "*¡Si, compañeros!*" "*¡No, compañeros!*" And all the dizzying exultation of hearts striving, embracing, in perfect union! "*¡No, compañeros!*" "*¡Si, compañeros!*" But this fraternal pride, this self-confidence, and this collective strength are in danger.

—9—

Awakened abruptly from a deep slumber, the young Dominican officer, Rafael Leónidas Trujillo, had begun taking potshots around his bedroom, convinced that Haitians had removed the Citadel from the sideboard where he had been keeping it safe. Some orderlies finally convinced him that the fortress had curled up under the parlor rug and that the Haitians, after a fruitless search, had gone on home.

After personally verifying this and congratulating himself on his keen vigilance, the Dominican officer went back to sleep with clenched fists.

And dreamed he was a cannon.

Rafael Leónidas Trujillo y Molina was stationed at the time in Azua. Always fond of tales told by poets in the folk tradition, he listened eagerly for themes that bolstered his political convictions. It was not unusual to run across an old fellow chewing on an unlit pipe in the barracks courtyard, spinning his yarns.

Oyez, oyez! The old poet:

"When Jean-Jacques Dessalines,[9] the Haitian commander in chief, entered Azua (lest we forget!), his chestnut horse walked breast-deep in blood. His men carried off horses, oxen, sheep, goats, donkeys, mules, geese, chickens, ducks, guinea fowls. At their passage flowers wilted, children went blind, and dogs got rabies."

The elderly storyteller, who had the tastes of a teenager, pulled from his satchel a publicity photo of an actress then in vogue — a ravishing beauty — to seek inspiration before continuing.

"The Haitian general wanted to throw out the French who occupied the eastern part of the island, our country, *La Dominicanie,* once and for all, thereby protecting Haitian independence from any offensive launched by Napoleon's troops from their bastions in the East."

The poet stopped talking. And kissed the actress.

These tales of the Eastern campaigns exasperated the young Dominican officer. He took a most particular dislike to General Jean-Pierre Boyer,[10] who had occupied his country for twenty-one years.

Trujillo slapped him: "You mixed the colors, Boyer!" He spat in his face: "You crucified the gardens." He put out his eyes: "You sewed up speech." He slashed his face with the point of a sword: "You made a mockery of love." He split him from head to toe: "You turned out the light." He carved him, sliced him, chopped him, minced him: "You crowned death." He trampled Boyer's leftovers in fury: "You turned history into a bone-yard, you made it an aberration!"

Suddenly calm, the young officer stationed in Azua admitted that the anonymous painter of the full-length portrait of Boyer was not without talent. Although he didn't much care for the dark circles under the eyes. Well, Boyer had probably been up late the night before. Trujillo couldn't get over it: he felt upset over ruining the full-length portrait of Jean-Pierre Boyer, President of Haiti.

And Trujillo dreamed of his own legend.

At that very same time, in a daily paper in Santo Domingo, someone had written:

"Dominicans still remember Faustin I,[11] Emperor of Haiti, who wanted to invade *La Dominicanie* so it would not fall into the hands of a European power. A saintly motive if ever there was one! But the Dominican people suffered too much from the campaigns of Faustin I to give him the benefit of any doubt whatsoever. Still, let us applaud the Haitian people who, bedazzled, kept him in power, but then, recovering their sanity, tossed him off his throne. They now desire our good fellowship."

This editorial created a groundswell of sympathy for Haiti in the Dominican Republic and a decline in vicious invective. Alphonse de Lamartine's four- or five-act play, *Toussaint Louverture,* played for a year at the Municipal Theater of Santo Domingo, six months at the Tropical Museum in Santiago de los Caballeros, three months at the Rowdy Pierrot in San Pedro de Macorís, one month at the Sorcerer's Apprentice in Baní, and three weeks at the Black Orchid in La Romana. The Society of the Friends of Haiti was founded with great fanfare. We acknowledged that we were a single people: the people of the island of Haiti.

Bitten by who knows what bug, Trujillo tore the newspaper to confetti in front of his soldiers, called the editor a lying opportunist and a defeatist of the deepest dye, swore that he would shortly have this traitor's hide plus shut down this dishrag and that he,

Trujillo, President of the D.R.,

In the judgment of the Council of the Secretaries of State,

In view of the law concerning the police, in regard to speech,

Whereas the exercise of sovereignty is delegated to three powers: the legislative, executive, and judiciary;

Whereas the law does not envisage any other power;

Whereas the press will not be cited as a power,

And it will be essential to put an end to abuses of power by journalists,

Will propose,

And the legislative body will pass, the following law:

Article 1 — Epidemic of silence in force throughout Dominican territory.

Article 2 — The present law will be published and executed etc. etc.

Trujillo harangued his men, exhorting them to civic action and patriotic ardor, while at the same time mysteriously asking them to believe in his karma.

The lieutenant was already showing signs of the Caudillo.

—10—

Standing in the middle of the street, Don Agustín de Cortoba, the representative of order, tackles the air. Armed with *la couline* — a long, thin, flat, gleaming machete for combat — he whirls around, sweeping up in his rotation the village steeple, his whitewashed house, the trees, the dust, the candy-pink porch of Preguntas, the dead dog, the flies, his own drunkard's mug, his bristling mustache, his beige belly. A head rolls at his feet. Taken by surprise, the air rears back at first, then ripostes. An arm moans. Some teeth grimace. Two fingers poke themselves up Don Agustín's nostrils. The air doubles over, then pounces, hissing. Don Agustín pants for breath. A yellowish drool drips down his chin. Don Agustín hiccups, returns to the fray. The air retreats. Confident of victory, Don Agustín advances boldly. The machete cuts, cleaves, chops, carves, slices, dices. Guts tumble at the feet of Don Agustín. A palpitating liver sticks to the skin of his stomach. The machete speeds up. The air huddles, a porcupine caught in a corner. Take that, and that! The machete amputates, mutilates, decapitates. Don Agustín sings, shouts, bellows, Don Agustín howls in the battle. Writhing nerves twine around his hams. And snip goes the machete, and snap goes the machete. One! Two! Hack, hew! The air cowers. Don Agustín sweats, swaggers, dashes here, darts there, advances, retreats, leaps, bounds. Each time he strikes, Emmanuela's long, slender legs grip, girdle, press, squeezing his huge beige body dry. And the machete cuts capers, turns somersaults. The machete pirouettes. Snicker-snack! And slashes, sunders, severs, shears. A bladder bursts. The air, abruptly, unleashes a multiplication of entrechats and — big surprise — strikes home. Don Agustín whimpers. Don Agustín slobbers. Don Pérez Agustín de Cortoba y Blanco gabbles like a goose. A vagina foams, contracted in pain. Slack-jawed, heart pounding, Don Agustín staggers around with Emmanuela's legs scraping his ribs. The machete snips, slits, struts its stuff. Princess, suzeraine, dowager, it visits its domain: bells, fields, houses, men's heads, women's hearts, and the laughter of children. Take that! Bisects, beheads. And that! Disjoints, dismantles, dismembers. A passing sunbeam is promptly chased down by Don Agustín and hanged from the top of a Spanish lime tree. Here are flowers, branches, fruits. Winded, Don Agustín stops, right in front of the house of Pedro Alvarez Brito, with heads clinging to his head, hands stuck to his hands, loins girdling his loins, two fingers up his nose, and hair in his left eye. And now here is my heart![12] Shivering, the air flings itself to the ground. Don Agustín is perspiring profusely as Emmanuela's long, slender legs go up and down him, lifting and rhythmically rocking him.

A rippling, rattling, crackling caterpillar of tufa, the main street of Elías Piña announces:

"Operation Haitian Heads has been going on now for over an hour. The scene is the Haitian-Dominican border; the characters: both peoples — more than 120,000 human beings interconnected through their languages, their pastimes, their dress, their customs, their environment — plus the machetes, of all shapes and sizes. Over by Dajabón, diligent machetes are cutting a current tally of more than thirty heads a minute; in Pedernales, a less hurried pace is racking up only eighteen. Here in Elías Piña, the machetes are in training with our head coach for Operation *Cabezas Haitianas,* Don Pérez Agustín de Cordoba, Grandmaster of the Clotted Blood. Be patient. We'll keep you informed of any new developments. Playing a bit part: the Haitian government. Enjoy refreshing Coca-Cola!"

And this unique radio — Elías Piña's main street — continues its broadcast with Tino Rossi singing "Under Paris Skies."

Don Agustín opens his mouth, releasing an endless stream of grasshoppers whose wings squeak *"¡Perejil!"* Ripped to rags, the air goes down for the count.

Don Preguntas Feliz arrives huffing and puffing, wiping his face with a putty-colored handkerchief. In great excitement, he whispers to Don Agustín. Then the two confederates turn their eyes to Adèle. She has almost finished rinsing the overalls, and now their smell of honest toil is really going to her head.

The representatives of power stare at me as if looks could kill. Can any human gaze be so inhuman? I saw Pablo Márquez fall in a burst of machine-gun fire last summer when Trujillo's Guardia crushed the workers' strike. The look he gave me held a flash of astonishment, but it was the look of a man. I saw Lucita Gómez clutch her abdomen as if to tear it open when the soldier brought the body of her son Renecito, a strapping young man, a journalist in Macorís, but the look she gave me was the dark, bewildered gaze of a grieving mother. There are lost, defeated eyes, buffeted by the four winds, the eyes of a lifer in prison; of a beggar mired in misery; the eyes of a dying patient turning away from the doctor; of a professional gambler who has placed a bad bet; the eyes of a startled child; the martyr's eyes of a simple plaster statue of Christ; the eyes of a rejected husband; of a fugitive tracked by the police; of a miser burning through his money. They're like the debris of human shipwrecks, but they are still the eyes of real people, hoping somehow to come safely into harbor . . .

As it happens, I, Adèle, I let myself be touched by a look.

Since that moment, my life has cleaved to that contact. I have found refuge there, the certainty of a presence, the gentle sweetness of domestication. From the first day Pedro looked at me, I enclosed myself within his joy, like pulp within a rind . . .

Ah! That day! A misty rain, so misty it was blue, hypocritical, haunting, skeptical, skinny, so blue it was misty, dreamy, insolent in its persistence, foolish, even childish, sticking out its tongue at you (Cuckoo!), without the slightest sign of letting up, a cheap actress underneath the gauzy, fluid garb, a rain that seemed almost earthbound, snooping so nosily into the slightest little thing, like coffee bushes, holes among the rocks, the crotches of trees, the nests of ortolans, flowerbeds, the grooves of corrugated-metal roofs, the nooks and crannies of the soul, and the melancholy of the human heart, a stubborn rain, a tiresome busybody, not hard but heavy, gnawing at the hours, soaking our high spirits, rubber-stamping our routines, batting its lashes as if just waking up, in a hurry but not quick, a confident sleepwalker, a coquette unspoiled by eccentricity, neutral, flaccid, silent, sarcastic thanks to all that quiet sniveling, as if it wanted to draw discreet attention to our rubbishy bits, our tiny disaster areas, revealing our scraps of exhaustion, just to amuse itself by tormenting us, both bold and shy, careless and serious, shameless and embarrassed, flighty yet not completely daft, unique without originality, a trivial event, the kind you get in the weather report *(an atmospheric depression for the next three days . . .)*, no high winds, no loud noises, posing no danger to small craft or butterflies or flowers or spiders, a humdrum, stay-at-home rain, at loose ends, from the neighborhood, a local character whose whims and foibles everyone knows, a seasonable rain, petty without realizing it, almost spineless, but who hangs on (a real duenna! Stands its ground, eyes peeled!), digging in, as if its mission were to pester, with an option to vex, harm, antagonize, yet seemingly so innocent, twiddling its billions of tiny fingers, girandoles, so misty they were blue, so blue they were misty, like young girls' dreams, and thus likely to lead to reveries, those stop-and-go inner voyages, in fact shooing you inside where it's warm, an abettor of bourgeois delights, of libidinous yawns, a slovenly rain, albeit limpid, clean, generous, yearning to be made in man's image, vulnerable in its doggedness, dramatic in its tremolo of laughter, but badly made-up, too blue for its grayish-green setting, and poorly suited, one might even say, for its role as a clown, without enough dignity in its jokes or drollness in its serenity, in short, sticking to the happy medium, a classic rain, cautious, quiet, at peace with its conscience (just a So-and-So rain!) and playing its part like a good girl, hoping for a smattering of polite applause before disappearing backstage — was drifting around, that morning, over Thomassique, in Haiti.

It was market day. The produce vendor stared hard at the big scale looming like a cross in the adobe arcade. The weights sitting in the two pans were arguing: "I'll be the one to decide the correct measure." "Nay, cousin, I should tip the balance!" The vendor dozed off with the rain in his eyes. The weights tangled in impossible wrangling: "I should!" "Uh-uh, cuz, *I* should!" With nothing to do, the scale was getting bored, so it started squeaking pianissimo. The vendor and the rain in his eyes sank deeper into his bamboo armchair. The arcade hunkered down. The rain was bivouacking in Thomassique, not a very showy rain, but eager to live up to its hallmark as a clinging and monopolizing drizzle. Across the way, the surveyor slept heavily, his measuring chain, stakes, and optical square down at his feet, while up at his plump, dirty neck, bugs were having a quiet field day. "We'll take two feet here," announced the stakes. "I'll cut back two meters there," countered the chain. "How I'd like to make everyone agree," said the square in ringing head tones. "I'd trim from here and there, round off corners, because made the way I am, I can really do things!"

The rain that day had definitely sworn eternal fealty to Thomassique. A rain with no idea how to plan, carry through, finish up. Coming, going, snooping around. Drizzle on the prowl! The surveyor slumped ever deeper into inertia. Sole signs of life: his raspberry shirt with small white polka dots and the almost unconscious slaps delivered to the bugs scaling his outlandishly fat neck. The surveyor had a goiter, which — incidentally — was why his wife had left him one Midsummer's Eve in Monte Cristi.

"I can't take it anymore, Señor Anastacio my husband, I just can't take it. I'm off."

"I've put everything aside for you, María my wife: house, lands, livestock, money, plus love . . ."

"And your neck, Anastacio my husband, your neck. A lemon. Tomato. Melon. I'm leaving your neck. And your ass. And your you-know-what."

Like a tall black taper with a pale flame, the Spanish priest stood on the threshold of the saffron-yellow chapel, next to a holy-water basin on a pedestal table covered with a spotless starched cloth embroidered in cross stitch. In the law office, it was hard to tell the notary from his decor: the filing cabinets, quill pens, seals, and inkwells echoed his seemingly cadaverous rigidity. Pinned down by the rain, Thomassique had seized up like Lot's wife. There wasn't one voice, not a single child's hoop, no beggar's song, not even the trickling of a fountain, still less the humming of a school. Everything was frozen. Motionless: the fabric merchant, his wares, the priest, his sacraments, the dentist, his clove oil, the *houngan,*[13] his nostrums, the rain, its dainty crystal fingertips. Even the silence had coagulated. Ah! That day . . .

Adèle changes the water in the basin, plunges in the overalls. That familiar heady smell of work. How stubborn it is! Honest sweat, bearing witness to our reasons for being, our mighty accomplishments: the sweat that throws bridges over rivers, links town, builds schools, masters energy, from darkness bringing light, from frustration, freedom, and from hatred, love. The sweat that puts trains on the right tracks, heals, spurs on endeavor, conditions and seasons life.

In the street, Don Agustín is busy burying the remains of the sunbeam. Here are flowers, branches, fruits. And now . . . After gorging themselves on dust, the children crawl away on their bellies. Here is my heart! One of them has grown spider's legs, crab claws, ginger rhizomes — who knows what! Hairy, viscous, twisted, he creeps up the gray walls of the chapel. Leaning on his pickax, Don Agustín salutes him solemnly; Emmanuela's long, slender legs make a grinding sound. A bell seems to have tolled. Once. Twice. Thrice. Adèle crosses herself, shakes out the overalls a few times, hangs them on the clothesline with the rest of the laundry. Satisfied, she contemplates her wash, and decides that Pedro's scent is definitely besieging her, possessing her, captivating her. She staggers, clutching the clothesline to steady herself. An orange shirt of coarse linen covers her face.

Ah! My man! Adèle feels a flash of heat. The orange linen shirt plays in her hair, grazes her lips, gently cradles her breasts, strokes her stomach, envelopes her, grips her waist, feels her thighs, presses her sex, presses, enters her, enters, penetrates her, fills her, explores her, possesses her. Ah! My man! He came out of the rain as if born of the rain. He alone moved amid the strange immobility of Thomassique. He was wearing his overalls, that day, and you could sense his laughter, his enthusiasm, his vitality . . . He came out of the rain like a church, a celebration, a harvest. Like — one might say — a peasant cooperative. Myriad little crystal paws frisked about him, swooping, gamboling, jingling.

Then galloped off.

He had known how to talk to the rain . . . which had gone home to the sky. And all at once buds were romping with the breeze, fruits gleamed on branches, flowers were in raptures, countless green birds squawked and sang to one another, while the surveyor, notary, produce vendor, *houngan,* priest, beggars, bells, and children's hoops leaped into action, measuring, verifying, selling, curing, preaching, panhandling, ringing, rolling. And when he ducked under the roof of the arcade where I had been sitting for more than five hours, when he arrived soaked but tall, strong, and confident, calling *"¡Buenos días!"* to everyone, a brand new sun burst out of him to shine on Thomassique. Country folk from the neighboring areas arrived leading mules laden with foodstuffs, fruits, and vegetables. Hundreds of Dominicans of all colors (brick, butter, cocoa, ebony) — riding red bulls with big white spots and garlands of wildflowers on their horns — waved broad-brimmed straw hats in the air, singing romantic *bachatas.* The rain had stopped. The fire of Pedro Brito Alvarez y Molina had burned it off. The market could begin.

It was on that day, in an arcade in Thomassique, that Pedro first set eyes on me.

Memory sees double when you're in love. A kind of drunkenness. Pedro has always insisted it was in Maribaroux that he first met me. Perhaps he wasn't paying any attention to me as he shook off the raindrops and remarked, "*¡Saludo!* What weather! The crops will rot."

"Everything is dead, *señor,*" I replied timidly.

"The sun will return."

"Really?"

"*¡Claro que sí!*" had promised the gigantic *señor.*

Since that moment, his presence has been joined to my life. Since that moment. Tenderly, Adèle pushes the orange linen shirt away from her face. She shivers lightly, agreeably; her belly tightens, her breasts swell, and a certain light flowers between her thighs. After a sudden shudder, her whole body relaxes, ecstatic. She feels refreshed, from her head to her womb. She turns pale!

Musing, Adèle goes inside the house. She can hear the pickax blows of Don Agustín digging a grave for the sunbeam he'd hanged by the neck until dead. Branches, fruits, pecked by birds. Outside: Elías Piña, deserted. "Hey, neighbor! Tell me — have you seen Don Pablo, *el profesor?*" Striking a rock, Don Agustín's pickax throws off sparks. Adèle lights the lamp to Our Lady, the Mater Dolorosa, in her portable shrine, and wonders why the Virgin hasn't smiled at her. And yet, the oil in the white china bowl is of good quality, and the yellow flame is burning blue at the wick. The smell of benjamin mingled with the scent of basil gives the room a taste of apples and flesh. Seized with terror, Adèle rushes out into the courtyard. "Neighbor! Have you seen *la santa? ¿La santa mía? ¿La mía santa? ¿Mía la santa?*" Don Agustín's pickax claws in the black soil laced with pink earthworms. Swaying its hips, the street performs conjuring tricks with long, flashing machetes — it curses, raves, murmurs, murders. Adèle rushes back into the bedroom like a whirlwind. The odor of apples and flesh stretches itself languorously; the flame in the white china bowl wavers, stands up, bows down, trembles, sputters, yellow burning blue at the wick. Adèle stares at the image of the Virgin. The image has lost its eyes. In place of the pale blue pupils quiver two indescribable little things. Two paws. Two chimneys. Two drops. Two.

Adèle races outside: "Hey! Neighbor! *Mira,* neighbor! Look! The Madonna's eyes are gone, off in the wild blue yonder, flown away home like black-and-yellow Our-Ladybugs. Neighbor, tell me! Where is my head? My *chiquita-haitiana-*from-Belladère's head. My head where the fires of day break. My headless head. My calamity-head. My boring old not-happy-enough head!"

The body of the sunbeam drops into the grave. Limp. Pitiful.

Adèle is overcome by exhaustion. A kind of flight of all

her limbs. Her right leg rolls in the dust beside the dog, now greenish-black with decay. Her left leg goes off to frolic around Don Agustín, who is tamping the sunbeam's body down into the soft ground. Adèle's left arm has snagged itself on something, she can't say what, but she has the feeling that it's barbed wire. An exasperating gnashing noise scrapes the air.

Channeling its radio, the street updates the news:

"In Azua Province, 908 heads; 819 in Santiago; in Pedernales, a sudden access of national fervor: 1,217! Dajabón is the winner, with a current head count of 15,208! (Pause.) Here in Elías Piña, in view of the training program, we started with the children: 128 males between the ages of eight and nine, 237 females between the ages of four and seven, nubile and pubescent, intended for the colonels. Unfortunately, we do not have a reliable statistical summary for that category of children. In any case, we will keep you informed. The operation is proceeding smoothly. Definite progress. *¡Saludo!* Gillette, the long-lasting blade that gives a close shave."

And the unique radio of Elías Piña's main street offers for consideration by its listeners an extract from the latest speech by Francisco Franco on "The Respect of Peoples for Their Leaders."

The vault of the firmament cracks.

Splitting, exfoliating, Adèle becomes half a body. I'm slipping. Ah! My man! The rain was blue, and went on forever. From the sky tumbled birds so green they seemed like torrents of water. Songs came from everywhere. And there were bells, fried fish, guitars, watermelons, hats, plus endless palaver!

Adèle measures the pangs of absence.

The street strikes up again in strident tones:

"The children's flesh is so tender that the machetes can't sink in — they slide instead of slicing, causing more painful bruises than outright wounds from direct hits. Therefore, as a humanitarian gesture, the *Cabezas Haitianas* Committee has stipulated that the throats of children be chomped with bare teeth. The tally for the moment: 8,286 children of both sexes have perished at the claws and fangs of the Guardia. The venture is going better and better from moment to moment. This evening, at The Eldorado, the film that's all the rage in the capital: *La Joie de Vivre!* Tonight's weather: cool all across the island."

And the only radio goes on the fritz with static.

The child atop the steeple screams loud enough to wake the dead: "*¡Perejil!*" The pickax plops the last clods of dirt on the corpse of the sunbeam. The entire village surges into view, as if propelled out of the earth, the sky, the air. Adèle is almost sweating delirium. "Neighbor! Where is the Virgin? *¿La santa mía?* Neighbor, I'm leaving!" The village laughs. Peal after peal of laughter, echoing even louder than the mad tolling of the bells. "Neighbor, I'm locking myself in!"

Firmly grasping his pickax with both hands, Don Agustín de Cortoba, pupils dilated, gets off on the tumultuous attentions of Emmanuela's long, slender legs.

—11—

One evening, in full finery and riding a chestnut thoroughbred at the head of more than two thousand men from his personal guard, Rafael Leónidas Trujillo y Molina (made chief of state by a Latin-American style *pronunciamiento*: a lightning-fast military coup that replaces an authoritarian government in the service of a *camarilla* with another authoritarian government in the service of a new coterie of the influential elite) struck a pose on the heights of San Francisco de Monte Plata simply to admire, among the lofty clouds of Northern Haiti, the silhouette of the Citadel. No one, either among his aides de camp or general staff, still less among his troops, saw, noticed, glimpsed, or even imagined any kind of a silhouette that by any stretch could possibly have been construed as the fortress of King Henri of Haiti. But he, Rafael Leónidas Trujillo y Molina, smiled strangely in the chilly darkness, caressing a firefly trapped in the emerald of his platinum ring. It was as if he had just signed a marriage contract between the thing-near-the-sky and himself, *el máximo jefe*. After gazing for a long while — as though contemplating eternity — at some mountain peak lost in the Haitian North, he withdrew, followed by his troops: forty-eight major generals with gold pompoms, on spirited steeds; fifty-three brigadiers with silver pompoms, on white chargers; three hundred and four colonels in dress caps, on Spanish jennets; eight hundred grenadiers and light cavalry with repeating rifles and burnished brass-plated breach-loaders, on mules; two hundred and thirteen sharpshooters with cartridge-pouches and shoulder-belts gallooned with gold, on bay mares; five hundred more grenadiers buttoned up tight in their brown linen paletots, on foot; five hundred and twelve light infantry in purple and azure, with beaver shakos trimmed with Moroccan velvet but no silk cords; seven hundred and two artillerymen in blue wool uniforms, dragging tiny iron cannons behind them. Fanfare: horns, bass tubas, trumpets, slide trombones, valve trombones, on thirty she-asses fitted with poplin saddle-cloths.

The shouting of the Dominican soldiers, the bucking and kicking of the restless mounts, and the warlike sounds of the brass so disturbed the woods, streams, roads, fires, blossoms, and birds that at the Caudillo's passage, an uneasy day dawned in the middle of the night.

That evening, the Generalissimo hurried home to the National Palace. He sensed that the monopoly of power demanded a myth that would not focus solely on his person, but would also affect both the political and sociological majorities of his entire country.

A myth! If he couldn't have the Citadel . . . A myth!

He sent immediately for his generals, liegemen, cronies. Held council. The single item on the agenda: to reveal to the

Dominican nation its true anthropological face.

They called in ethnographers, ethnologists, sociologists, historians, linguists, even statisticians. They deliberated. Some, experts on the question, spoke right up: "The Dominican nation is a product of the black African and red American races." Quite beside the point. "Simplistic propositions," declared the voice of authority.

They reopened the inquiry. Brought in works on semantics, thematics, semiotics, dermatology, philosophy. Studies of the overall situation, a *Treatise on the Education of Nations.* They beavered away. Sweated like pigs. And discovered: "The human race is Dominican!" A rather timid minority proposed: "It's both human and Dominican!" Who? Who knows who. Or what.

To control his emotions, Rafael Leónidas Trujillo y Molina cracked his knuckles. (Even megalomaniacs, it seems, have nerve-racking habits.) Trujillo imposed silence — sepulchral — upon the learned gathering, stared off into the distance, and announced: "We are the *blancos de la tierra!*" His audience wavered at first, then broke into applause: "*¡Viva los blancos límpidos de la tierra!* Long live the pure whites of the earth!" Unanimity coalesced around this godsend. Congratulations were in order. General agreement that Dominican anthropological science had hit a bull's eye. Thanks to the boss's brainstorm. Printers, engravers, draftsmen, lithographers — even ladies of the evening, for the esthetic point of view! — were promptly summoned. They slaved away on stone, lead, paper, cardboard, day, night. Then both the Air

Force's biplanes showered the land with "*¡Blancos de la tierra!*" vignettes, prints, and leaflets. The promotion of the myth had begun.

The Dominican people, however, peering at, studying, and exploring themselves, wondered, "What's this '*Blancos de la tierra*' business?" And went back to their merengues, their cockfights, their songs, laughter, jobs, amours, follies, furies, hopes, and miseries.

As for Trujillo, his conversation sparkled: *¡Blancos de la tierra!* "It will be just as good as the Citadel," he mused dreamily. "A myth for a phantasm!"

Snatching up the slogan, rightwing intellectuals tried it out in art and literature. Poems, rondeaus, odes, sonnets, hymns poured forth, while the ballads called *romanceros* flourished in abundance. Public places broke out in rashes of paintings classical, baroque, modern, and miscellaneous; historical theses were born; plays popped up like dandelions and were staged in the capital, provincial cities, small towns, rural backwaters. Every day at first light, carts laden with theatrical impedimenta and escorted by thespians headed out into the countryside. Performed on makeshift stages, the most unexpected scenes amazed the delighted public from dawn to dusk.

Here's one of the most popular playlets of the time:

"A woman gives birth to a male infant in a rural marketplace. The newborn is neither very dark nor very pale. From a certain angle, he looks chocolate. From another, coffee-colored. To the naked eye he's saffron yellow, even more so under a magnifying glass. At sunrise, he's pumpkin. At sunset, closer to peanut. In the arms of his first cousin, he's like burnt bread. From the back, he's this. From the side, he's that. Everyone gathers to discuss this phenomenon. Along comes a senator of the republic, as jolly, pink, and tubby as a porcelain doll, a skilled anthropologist, a Doctor of Melanin, who lays his hands on the infant's head and intones: "*¡Tú eres blanco de la tierra!* You are a *blanco de la tierra!*" The chorus choruses back: "*¡Tú eres blanco de la tierra!*" Voilà.

A miracle. Hosanna! From the bottom of our balls!

Rafael Leónidas Trujillo y Molina, the Dominican head of state, defined his nation neither by its daily life nor by its collective aspirations, but by the color of its skin.

Leftwing intellectuals pointed out that the slogan had been launched to divert attention from the poverty of the people. "An escape-hatch," "Sleight-of-hand," "A complete mishmash," trumpeted the opposition media.

Unaware of these debates on the left and right, the Dominican people continued to wonder: "*Blanco de la tierra* — just what does it mean?" Double voilà.

—12—

Adèle buries her head in her hands. Her finger-joints crack: "*¡Perejil!*" Padre Ramírez's black cassock, the olive-drab truck, the young man with his fingers worn down by music, the crazy bells, the children with dusty eyes, the dead dog, soap bubbles, flies, bonfire, the charred hanks of women's hair, the two toothless trollops, hunchbacked and verminous, the drums, holy water, flutes, cymbals, the old suicide, the lost eyes of the Virgin prance, dance, wriggle, cackle, gesture and grimace, embrace, and parade down the street chanting: "*¡Perejil!*" Adèle vomits. At her feet swarm countless unspeakable things shed by Don Agustín, who has been standing unnoticed before her for some time. And who orders her to say "*¡Perejil!*" Adèle stammers. The *l* has fled into her uvula. The *e* has trod on the *i*. The *j* has frozen up. The *p* is bumping into the *r*, stifling it. Adèle's mouth opens painfully. An almost inhuman sound wobbles out. Don Agustín swells, shoots upward, hoisted by Emmanuela's long, slender legs, until his noggin is level with the raptor's. The two heads confer. Then Don Agustín shrinks, descends between Emmanuela's legs. His enormous beige belly pops out from beneath his black sports shirt. His teeth champ and gnash: "*¡Perejil!*" Adèle mumbles "*¡Perejil!*" Her tongue coils. Her gums grow hot and puffy. The whole word squeezes into her throat with a gurgle that must hurt. Then the young woman's limbs come to the rescue of her voice. But the left leg has switched places with the right one — and they're squabbling: "I'm going first." "Forget it, me first!" Don Agustín bellows "*¡Perejil!*" Snarls "*¡Perejil!*" Adèle tries one more time. The letters get mixed up, have a shoving match, fall to pieces, down the hatch. Adèle leaves, hoists the flag, turns off the faucet, and caresses Pedro, handling him, turning him this way and that, the way she did before he left at sunup.

"The dawn is dangerous, Pedro," she had said.

"Don't get upset, Adèle. I must speak to the others."

"But dawn kills, its thorns are hidden, but dawn kills. It's called the dawn fever, just as there is flower fever, saint's fever, spring fever — "

"*Está bien,* Adèle, I'll be careful. But you, don't you forget your sedative."

"They hand out pills like candy, but my head's all colors of gray."

"They're good for your nerves, you know that!"

"My nerves are in a state, as the saying goes."

"A state of beauty, I'd say."

"In my body of gray skies and patchy sunshine, Pedro?"

"In your flourishing, beautiful, black woman's body, sweetheart!"

"Sweet-talker! Off with you, *Dios te bendiga.*"

"Remember to take your sedative!"

"And you, watch out for the soft blaze of dawn!"

"Adiós, chiquita mía."

The sunbeam sags deeper into its grave. The child tolls the bells, his rhizomatous fingers gripping the ropes that set them pealing left and right in the tiny white wooden steeple. A brazen, bone-rattling ringing wings out over the roofs. The sky cracks. Elías Piña is once again in adoration of Trujillo: "Saint, saint, saint, anoint thy people, thy nation, thy bride!"

The raptor (to be honest, no one knows what it is) has girded itself with shadows, tipping the strutting sun and all its medals into darkness.

Don Agustín is lapping noisily. Emmanuela is undulating. The *negrita*'s nipples stiffen. Don Agustín starts slobbering. Emmanuela wriggles. The *negrita*'s belly snaps. Don Agustín stutters. Emmanuela rears. The *negrita*'s body leaps. Don Agustín collapses, pumped dry. Dazed, he rubs a flabby hand over his damp fly.

A crackling:

"Attention, please! There has been a request to speed up the operation. There is absolutely no call to poeticize the accumulation of heads, along the lines of 'falling petals' or 'falling stars' — typical naive metaphors we must banish from the Dominican nationalist vocabulary. Let them fall by the hundreds of thousands every second (mown down like hay, exactly): we remain unaffected. When you pull up weeds, you don't pay attention to the cicadas' song. Make way for the serenity of machetes, the spilling of blood! (Pause.) While we're on the subject: 18,203 heads in Dajabón.

For children, teeth and claws; results, positive; *método: ¡Hasta luego!* Flash! After the death of Sanjurjo,[14] General Francisco Franco has become the uncontested master of Spain. Today our president has sent him a message for the occasion. Listerine protects and whitens your teeth!"

And the only radio on the main street begins to prattle about the benefits of fluoride in dental hygiene.

Leaving Emmanuela's bed, Don Agustín roars: "*¡Perejil!*" As if abruptly inspired, he dashes toward a kitchen garden adjoining the old gray presbytery with the slate roof. In the twilight, the blowsy heads of cabbage throw out their chests; the leeks draw themselves up like soldiers. He's looking for something or other. The lettuces open their hearts. The pink-and-white radishes show off in the tender shade of the celery. Suddenly overjoyed, Don Agustín pulls up a bright green tuft of parsley and brandishes it like a trophy before dashing back. A rustle of wings sets the wild thyme shivering. *(Adèle sees the machete coming,)* Don Agustín waves the parsley, squeaking: "*¡Perejil!*" *(sees it teasing passersby,)* Chortling: "*¡Perejil!*" Mewing: "*¡Perejil!*" Farting: "*¡Perejil!*" Adèle's mouth opens. Elías Piña piles inside with a crash, the village's laughter still rolling over the roofs. *(sees it skipping rope,)* Don Agustín's machete rises, sucks up darkness, *(sees it slip between her breasts.)* and whirls around, carrying along in its windmilling the chiming bells, *(Adèle hears the machete talking to her,)* the crawling, spinning spiders, the blinding, stifling dust, *(telling her stories,)* the stretching, upsetting street, *(imitating the ocean.)* Father Ramírez, the whitewashed house, the blind Virgin, the fields, the stars, and the machete spins in circles, gets itself together, growing stronger from the darkness, and shoots all the way up to the thing, *(Adèle senses the machete is running out of breath,)* consults the object, swears to obey the orders to slice-and-dice, shrieks with laughter, savors its feast of flesh, *(sweating over its work.)* asks for a drink, carouses, gaily greets the entire village, which it demands bear witness to its redoubtable striking force and tempered steeliness, then pledges fresh allegiance to the System ("Anoint, anoint thy people, thy lamb!") and flits about, warming the hand of Don Agustín — to which the machete gives confidence, guarantees power, promises a role in the grand finale plus the conveyance of kind regards to the *Cabezas Haitianas* Committee — and, smelling blood, pirouettes, prances, swanks around, confers again with that flying thing, coordinates, plans, returns to earth, kicks up its heels, plays the fool, reassures Don Agustín's hand, observes, reasons, hesitates: "Am I cut out to cut off heads? What will the grass say? The boles of oaks? The old mango trees, sages of the Sierra?" Then, impulsively — "I am my own master, as I am of death" — the machete opts for the Reason of State, the purity of the Dominican nation, its authenticity, specificity, originality, remembers it's the champion of the *blancos de la tierra,* persuades itself that ocher must snuff out black, leach it out, so that from Bahoruco to Monte Cristi all will be yellow or white (mostly white) like the dawn rallying its people of light, white like the foaming crests of waves breaking into doves of water. And hop! The machete makes up its mind, *(Adèle imagines it as a train, a snake in the night, a dragon,)* comes to a conclusion, and falls on the back of Adèle's neck! *(a vapor, a doll, a locust.)*

Aghast, the young woman's head opens eyes in which floats a blue rain, so blue it's misty, so misty it's blue. "Hey, neighbor! Have you seen my man? He went into the dawn. My man, Pedro Brito, the worker at San Pedro de Macorís, the husband of the dawn! Did you watch him grow up? Neighbor! *¡Dime por favor!*"

The sunbeam is seeping deeper and deeper into the clayey soil, amid the pink miracle of the earthworms, the village's hearty laughter, the din of the bells rung by the spider recovering its human form: paws with dirty nails, a shaved head with mauve scabs, the swollen belly of a suckling pig.

Elías Piña's main street lets out a squeak:

"By mistake, the Dominican Guardia has killed more than five hundred of its own peasants on the banks of the Guayamuco River. Although we regret this incident, we must condemn all discontented rumors, as well as any hint of controversy. Buy Dominican: Bermudez, the macho rum!"

The sole radio hiccups as the power goes off for just a second.

"Neighbor, he had to go see the others . . . About joining forces. My head can hardly remember. But Pedro went to see his comrades to . . . Yes . . . Join forces. With the dawn. And the colors."

Don Agustín de Cortoba scratches his paunch, a sign that he is thinking deeply. He cannot understand why a head as lovely as Adèle's can't properly pronounce the word *perejil.* "It must be a head on the run. A flyaway head," he concludes aloud, clearly pleased with himself, and then improves on that: "A departed head. A head unworthy of posthumous honors," he winds up, beaming.

With a smile of happy idiocy, he returns to the long, slender legs of Emmanuela.

—13—

Chicha Calma, the orange *guagua* with the pale green hood, gobbles up the rosy air of a Dominican sunset strongly scented with cane molasses. Sneezes. Clears her throat. I, Chicha Calma, the *guagua* of the border, I carry the cities and villages on my tires. I recognize their particular smells a hundred leagues in any direction (Ouanaminthe smells like café au lait) and can distinguish their individual refrains. From beyond the mountains, plains, valleys, I sense their peace or their distress. The wind, my constant companion, brings me detailed up-to-the-minute reports on their doings. Even the stream crossings sometimes whisper to me stories about the border people that I, Chicha Calma, do not find funny and file permanently away on the spot, being rather reserved by nature. The *guagua* jolts. The driver is dozing. His head lolls from left to right, leans forward, tips backward. Shakes itself. "Hey there! *¡Ten cuidado!* Be careful!" Drools. Sags. The driver's head dreams of a heaping plate of kilometers. From its earliest childhood it has done nothing but gobble kilometers. From La Romana to Monte Cristi. His Dominican driver's head. From Sánchez to Higüey. Kilometers of asphalt. Over mountains. Kilometers of beaten earth.

Across fords. His auburn head, scarred by smallpox. Kilometers of tufa, of mud. Through thickets. With appetizers of *muchachitas'* laughter and the back-slaps of amigos, "Put 'er there, *compadre! ¡Una viudita te espera!* You've got a merry widow waiting for you!" Through quagmires. *¡La cabeza de la Lucía!** And the driver's head nuzzles a hairy armpit, nestles between two big breasts, plunges down the highway of a sleek belly. Fumbles. Through narrow valleys. "*¡Cuidado compadre!* You're nodding off!" And the driver's mustachioed head stomps on the accelerator. Chicha Calma's entire orange tinplate body creaks, smokes, backfires, stalls.

Pedro Brito is upset to find himself still on the road back to Elías Piña from the factory, especially since he's not bringing much home to Adèle . . . Two years! For two years he has been exploring that woman's body, camping on her ground, resting in her peace, sleeping in her safety. For two years! He has been the taproot of a life, the confession of a soul, the arousal of desire, her appetite, her quest, her pillar of strength, her clairvoyance, her shield, her audience, her aid, her proper setting, her code, her vision of the future, her plan, the refuge of her sorrow. For two years! He has been supported by the tenderness and abundance of that woman. And now here he is, Brito, returning to Elías Piña without anything reassuring for that same woman. Without her fair share.

"Listen, Guillermo Sánchez! The word is that machetes

---

* By the head of Saint Lucy!

are killing hard in the cane fields. Seven machetes for one Haitian head. No — the latest news says fifteen, eighteen machetes for a single Haitian head. Even twenty! Carefully sharpened, handed out to anyone who can say *'perejil'* the right way. Secret orders, rallying cry, official policy, the law — all demand that every Dominican arm chop off at least a hundred Haitian heads. Guillermo Sánchez y Santana! You are the voice of the factories: speak, I beg you. The compassion, friendship, courage, and devotion that cynics call humanist nonsense are your personal hallmarks, Guillermo Sánchez y Santana! You have never kept silent before a pleading voice in trouble, or turned your back on public action. You are always in the thick of things, for minor problems or major crises. To you a task is first and foremost something to be carried out. And it's only afterward that one can measure the size and challenges of the job you've done. That's one of your basic principles as a man and labor leader. Your generosity does not hamper your strength as a revolutionary, but on the contrary gives wisdom to your political decisions and earns the respect of your comrades in arms, justifying their confidence and enhancing your reputation. During the strike in San Francisco de Monte Plata, that's why your word carried particular weight in the negotiations and led the way to an agreement. The workers won their case. The Company granted them a decent raise. The men shouted *'¡Viva Guillermo Sánchez y Santana!'* But when the applause began, you melted into the crowd of overalls as if your worth depended only on their fraternal bond. 'They are their own strength, *compadre* Brito,' you told me.

"They are the heart, you are the head. In our struggle, despite appearances, we must have faith in knowledge. Oh yes, yes, Guillermo Sánchez y Santana, *mi amigo!* Take it from me, Pedro Alvarez Brito y Molina."

"Look at these men, how they shout. They don't keep their feelings behind shutters. They're like children. We are above all an exuberant people, *compadre* Brito! Exuberant, *coño!*"

"*¡Bueno!* But Sánchez, for us you are the authority. Do you agree we must still have an authority, after all? *¡Coño!*"

"*¡Qué sí, compañero! ¡Claro que sí! ¡Cómo no!* Of course!"

"*¡Entonces!* So! You are the authority most devoted to the common good. *¡Entonces!* Yes or no?"

"I'm not saying no. But we've got a long road ahead before our hearts will all beat in time . . . to reason, old friend. Brito, we are a people . . ."

"Exuberant, I know! But you and I are both labor leaders. You know the resources a people has, *¿sí o no?*"

"My dear Brito, history is the dough of peoples: it makes all sorts of loaves — you taught me that."

"There'll be some good ones!"

"*¡Seguro, compadre!* Shake on it. I won't say no. Shake on it. *¡Seguro, amigo!*"

"And you, Alfredo Peredo! Will you let the beast put death on the throne? Will you leave the widow's cry unanswered? The child abandoned? Old folks helpless? I come in the name of the coffee we've shared, the cockfights we've watched together at the *gaguerres,* in the name of arms that know what it's like to cut cane . . . I come in the name of the sweat of working people."

And the workers had gathered to listen.

"We all know the song of the cane. It shows our mettle at dawn, measures our exhaustion at sundown. We are the children of the cane. We share its harsh flaws as well as its succulent goodness."

That's what the factory workers are like. That's how our meetings always go. And that's how we talked today to try working out ways of saving as many Haitian heads as possible from the massacres. But our means are limited, and our young organizations are weak and inexperienced. It will be a long time before we can effectively resist the powers that be.

Over there, on the other side, on Haitian soil, lingers a scrap of sunshine. Pedro would love to take it like a sheet of coarse linen. To cover himself. Hide himself. He reaches out. The scrap of sunlight, as if frightened, goes marooning* into the mountains across the way. Night falls on the island in the racket of the anolis' chirping cries and the smell of the cane fields. I am the tree, Adèle is the bark. The same sap flows through us both. The fruits that will come of us will have the same flavor, the same tartness, the same sweetness, the same lingering taste on the palate, so truly have I lived in her and

---

* Derived from the American Spanish *cimarrón* (wild, unruly), "maroon" originally meant a fugitive black slave in the West Indies, and "to maroon" was to run away into the hills.

she received me. But Trujillo! . . . Is it acceptable that one night, among the ashtrays, the empty, half-full, and unopened bottles, between the international news and the weather forecast, the breaking of a glass and the scratching of a belly, a kick at a dog and a rumbling gut, a busy toothpick and a servant's scolding, a bug bite and a belch, a random word and the reconvening of the court, on paper bearing the official seal of the *República Dominicana — Dios, Patria, Libertad — Año Mil Novecientos Treinta y Siete,* should be decreed the decapitation of more than fifty thousand people of all ages, of all kinds, of all classes: libertines, husbands, churchgoers, delinquents, tradespeople, manual laborers, factory workers, tramps, farmhands, artisans, apprentices, paupers, construction workers, foremen, dotards, sprightly oldsters, helpless invalids, smartypants, butterfingers, jerks, strapping youths, brains, dopes, old fogies, teenagers, brats, pubescent boys, marriageable girls, and grandmas?

"Federico Carpenter! Sergio Nuñez! Estrellita Manuel!"

I know! It's generally in such surroundings, among the cigars and the reasons of State, that the snags in life, the foul blows, the outrages, the sneak attacks on decency are plotted; it's between a black coffee and a tired sigh, between a typist's smile and some patriotic blather that the bad tempers, fanaticism, and intrigues are hatched; it's between the usual remarks and a cold supper that markets are rigged, crooked bargains cooked up, that hatreds, jealousies, and schemes are brewed; and it's between a handshake and a mention of the nation's conscience, between a game of cards and praise for a certain make of car, amid the gallery openings, wagers, reproaches, intermissions, cigarette butts, promises, compliments, rendezvous, soccer matches, jokes, criticism, folderol, Nobel prizes, and words of love, between afternoon tea and the caresses of a cat, between chalk and cheese that the stinking machinations and death sentences spew forth, and the foaming filth of genocides. Yes, I know — I'm just a worker! My education is limited because the life I was handed hasn't given me the chance to develop my intelligence, but I've seen my share of human scum at work and in daily life.

"Abel Cedio! Roberto Mateo! Angela Cepeda! I've come in the name of the strike we organized last year."

When slogans flew, voices shouted, bullets slew.

"Pablo Colón! Perceval Rodriguez! I appeal in the name of good, honest sweat."

And the workers had gathered together. The flesh of workers is common flesh. It gleams red in the light of dawn. Closes up shop at night. Always faithful to what it firmly believes, it cannot believe that night should lay down the law. The flesh of workers is both a political statement and the rattle of chains. It has the force of law when the law has foundered.

That's what workers are like. That's how we talked today. But we admit that our organization is fragile, and needs shoring up.

A bald, middle-aged man with a pale complexion lights his pipe. The scent of bergamot fills the *guagua*. The driver's head brakes: a little *india* girl wants to go peepee. Pedro takes the opportunity to relieve himself as well. Someone in the *guagua* strikes up a merengue, then falls silent. In the distance, over Elías Piña, a section of sky crumbles in a shower of fiery shards that collide, shatter, ricochet pell-mell. Somebody says: "*¡Ya comienza!* Now it begins!" Makes the sign of the cross. Repeats: "*¡Ya comienza!*" Repeats the sign of the cross. The middle-aged man empties his pipe. "I will not add my fire to their witches' sabbath." A young woman chants "*perejil*" to herself. The *r* is treading on the heels of the *l*. Hunched over, the young woman weeps softly. With each quiver of her shoulders, she gives off a faint perfume of roses. Like Adèle, when she saw the thing. Adèle with her crown of thorns! Adèle! It was at the market in Maribaroux that I saw Adèle for the first time.

"Lovely day, isn't it, *señorita!*"

"Indeed, a good day for the market, monsieur," she replied.

"You're not from around here?"

"I come here every Tuesday, but I'm from Belladère."

"Ah! A pretty village. I have a friend in Belladère, Emmanuel Eustache. Do you know him?"

"Belladère's a rather big place, you know, *señor!*"

"There are also some very beautiful girls where you come from."

"You shouldn't say that, *señor!*"

"You, for example. Such pretty skin!"

"People do say I smell like citronella."

("What a girl!" Pedro had murmured. "One minute with her, I'm off in the clouds! Barely fifteen years old! This is seventh heaven!")

"My nose would be happy to check," I ventured to say.

"The sky is clouding over, don't you think, monsieur?"

"Believe me, *señorita,* this isn't the time of year for bad weather. True, the sky is overcast — a southwest wind, perhaps, but it isn't the season yet, I can assure you. And after all, with you, it's summertime!"

("Yah! What a line!" she must have thought. "He's one of those guys who set young girls' windmills turning. *La madre mía* warned me about your sweet nothings: Go flirt with someone else, m'sieur! Off with you, *bigotes de gato!* Tomcat!")

But: "Oh, m'sieur!" was all she said.

Hundreds of *muchachos* were arriving astride cows with long horns garlanded with yellow wildflowers. The boys swatted their broad-brimmed straw hats at parrots swooping down from the sky in such numbers that the air turned green. Parrot green. Flapping, fluttering, screeching green . . . The sky was squawking, too, pitching and rolling lustily with the darting cries of the birds. The *muchachitos* kept waving them away with their hats, but the parrots kept coming back, more and more attracted by the boys' cries: "*¡Bueno! ¡Ya! ¡Cómo no!*" The *muchachitos* eventually gave up, and the jolly concert of human voices plus the chatter of ever so many green birds played merrily on, broadcast past the woods, road, clouds, the market haggling, insults, swaying hips, glinting glassware, the Pentecostal pastor's service, the drums, the pharmacist's glass jars, the National Lottery tickets, the garage mechanic's axle grease, the butcher's cleaver. Naked black children with gleaming skin showed off reed baskets of mauve hairy crabs brandishing their lustrous, menacing claws. Past the billboards with government publicity: Water mains laid in major construction; Free democracy soon — for everyone; Affordable health care; Mass campaign against illiteracy next March. Past the backbiting gossip, the gospel of the Catholic priest, the lotto players, the man with the trained mongooses, the drunks, the jostling, the sweat.

"Pedro Brito, you said? I know a Pedro Brito in La Loma, another in Banica, a third one in Ouanaminthe, a fourth in . . ."

"There are plenty of Britos at the border. It's the same for Mateos, Nuñezes, Espaillats. Me, I'm from Elías Piña," I told Adèle.

"I was there once — a puce-colored town that smells like tamarind."

"And you?"

"Me?" countered Adèle, strangely surprised.

"What do mere mortals call such a lovely creature?"

"Adèle!"

"Perfect! Adorable Adèle!"

I thought her scent was more like morning dew, as if her body had been rubbed with a garden.

"Some call me Douce Folie — but only my closest friends."

"You have the name of a perfume."

("Ah! This guy!" she must have thought. "Trouble! A runaway truck — get out of its way if you want to save your skin! Me, I keep my eyes open. *La madre mía* warned me.")

But: "Soon you'll be saying my body is like a pretty melody, monsieur," she said, smiling coquettishly.

Heavy quarters of bloody beef hung from the tops of ten groaning pulleys lined up along a wall of green concrete. Perplexed customs officials wondered about the provenance of the poultry. Haitian or Dominican? The fowls themselves just kept on cackling. On all sides welled up boisterous laughter, calls, yells, the shrieking of whistles. Sitting on the bare ground, inscrutable *houngans* sold their wares: bowls of gray paste, snake vertebrae, chunks of pig's feet, dried hummingbird hearts, divinatory potions in bottles, *mombin* gum, thunderstones,[15] and all the rest of the paraphernalia.

"From now on, Tuesday will be a sacred day for me, Adèle."

"This market is my favorite of all those along the border."

"I'll wait for you here next week."

"I came in hopes of seeing a friend of my mother's about a saucepan. Perhaps I'll be lucky enough to find her next Tuesday."

"Tuesday, the sky will be wearing all its medals."

("Hmm! He doesn't waste time," she probably thought. "He's no truck, he's an airplane. A woman would be foolish to breathe his hot air! She'd be dizzy in no time. And fall right over.")

"I promise," she whispered.

"Don't forget, Adèle: a promise is a promise!"

"I always forget. But this time, I'll remember."

("Monsieur," she must have been thinking, "my head's a bit cracked (they say), but I don't think I'll be swept off my feet so easily." Still, *gallo dominicano* that I am, I cockily pushed things a little further:)

"I promise to bewitch you, Adèle."

"The weather's definitely changing. Or my head's imagining things . . . Oh, well! You were saying, *señor*? Señor Brito, wasn't it?"

("With that head on her shoulders," Brito said to himself, "she really can spin the sky completely around — that head and her garden perfume, as if she had all the aromas of the island at her command. *¡Qué mujer!* A real queen of hearts!")

"We'll have a mild night, with starshine everywhere, Señorita Adèle," I stammered, dazzled by my own flowery language.

. . . Past the stray dogs, the squabbles, the vendors' displays, the rural policeman's badge, the soap, sugar, kerosene. Past the flying rumors (independent of all newspapers, magazines, and radios), past the jamborees, shady deals, past the life of both peoples, their acceptance, their refusal. Minor officials dashed frantically around collecting taxes: rump of one fowl, ten centimes; haunch of one billy-goat, twenty centimes; measure of red beans, five centimes; basin of offal, two gourdes. The dentist waited impatiently with his clove oil at the ready. And their meddling schemes, their resilience, their tacit understandings. Past the rain, the sunshine (since heads of state care nothing for fair or foul weather), hills and dales, disagreements, sorrows, choices, chicks, calves, cows, pigs. Dusty horses tethered to stout stakes flicked their tails at blowflies and other pests. A pleasant and almost famishing smell of frying tickled noses everywhere. Squatting on a reed mat out in the tropical sun, the village madwoman, a mass of rags the color of ashes, kept licking the tip of her right index finger and pointing north, south, east, west, mechanically turning round and round to find out just where the wind was coming from.

"Give me your hand, Adèle, to seal your promise."

"I've seen you before, you know, at Thomassique, in the rain, *señor*."

("What fate has set him on my path again? The first time I saw this man in Thomassique, the earth fell away beneath my feet. I felt giddy with inexplicable delight, or confusion," she must have . . .)

Quick, keep the conversation going: "I'm fond of that market, too. That's where I usually buy my tobacco."

"I know all the markets on the border. I've already been as far as Fort-Liberté in the northeast, and Pedernales at the southern tip."

"And your hand, Adèle?"

"I will keep my promise and speak to you."

("This man! Yow! A real live wire! Watch out, Adèle," she must have warned herself.)

"I accept, my dear!" I exclaimed. I came right out with it: "The sooner the better!"

. . . Past the decisions of the powers that be, past daydreams, disappointments, madness and folly. With Adèle, her scents, her pearly teeth, the *muchachitos,* the kaleidoscope of parrot-greens, the cows with blossom-bedecked horns, the hats, the mountain, human joie de vivre, the sky, the two republics, their mingled presence in Maribaroux, at a country market. O Maribaroux!

Since that moment, Adèle has joined her daily life with mine. A gift I eagerly accept.

—14—

The Citadel was sleeping cradled in a thin basin of clouds. The sky above it was brooding on eternity. Alone in the night, on the rugged terrain of Puerto Plata, sitting astride his blood bay, the Caudillo gazed at the fortress. He wanted it. It was settling itself deeper and deeper into the night sky when, awakened by the glare of a sudden moon, it appeared, drowsing in all its mass of stone. Seeing it like that, royal in that black and white universe, the Caudillo was stirred to the depths of his soul, blinking, muttering, and shaking from head to toe like a child in front of a forbidden gadget. He wanted to have the Citadel on his good Dominican soil, atop Entre Los Ríos (2440 meters), or Monte Tina (3190 meters). To obtain it, what could possibly have been asked of him that he would not immediately have given? He would have mortgaged the nation to have it in his room, in his bed, with its three hundred and sixty-five bronze cannons, its cisterns, dungeons, stables, archives, its barracks that could house ten thousand men. He wanted it in his body, in his nights, in his amours. He wanted it very, very much and suffered cruelly at not possessing it. Perched on his blood bay, he contemplated it for hours on end. Intimidated by his gaze, the fortress hid among the clouds for a long time. But when — inevitably — it rose with the sun, its forehead bathed in sparkling dew-drops and a golden glow, the Caudillo's heart would send up a hymn so powerful, so wrenching, that the inhabitants of Puerto Plata, Terrier-Rouge, and Ouanaminthe must have heard it every day at dawn for years on end.

The Citadel fled further and further from Trujillo's dream. But although the phantasm was frightened, the myth was holding its own.

In Ciudad Trujillo,[16] San Pedro de Macorís, Barahona, Baní, Puerto Plata, throughout the Dominican Republic, technocrats, bureaucrats, psychologists, psychoanalysts, judges, Freemasons, inspectors, and ambiguity experts denounced the "mirror syndrome."

Every day, fourteen out of fifteen Dominicans spent hours consulting mirrors. Studying and taking stock of themselves.

Anyone who saw himself as light brown, a betwixt-and-between brown, could breathe easy; he fit the anthropologico-Trujillonian criterion: he was a *blanco de la tierra*. Or pretty close to it. Suitable for social advancement. But anyone who found he was one-quarter, or one-third, or one-half, or completely black . . . got really worried. He was destined to suffer.

Sometimes, though, the mirror would reflect you as a freshwater turtle, a painted basket, a child's balloon, a cucumber, a coconut, a tiled roof, a sewing machine, a stick of barley sugar, or a pink flamingo with an umbrella for a head. The Dominicans concluded that the mirrors were having nervous breakdowns. Ophthalmologists, psychiatrists, psychics, film directors, first-aid workers, and economic prognosticators all confirmed the popular diagnosis: mirrors throughout the nation were going gaga.

This was a godsend for importers, who ordered new mirrors from North America, Europe, Asia, Africa. Thousands of boats, small crafts, vessels, ships, ocean liners, frigates, and corvettes flying a rainbow of flags came into port, dropping anchor ten minutes apart and laden fore, aft, and everywhere with mirrors in which the sky and its seagulls had managed to become trapped.

The Dominicans got all the mirrors they wanted and then some. The miniaturized American mirrors were placed on the tips of shoes; the square European ones at the front doors of houses; the beveled Asian ones on ceilings; the oval African ones under the beds.

Morning, noon, and night people looked at themselves in mirrors, but deep down, they didn't trust them. Someone who had seen himself as snow-white fifteen minutes earlier would detect a café-au-lait tint an hour afterward. Sometimes people wound up as jugs, accordions, skylarks, or varying amounts of horsepower. And lost all faith in themselves, their specificity, their *roots*.

A beautician announced that she had solved the problem. She had, it seems, perfected a product made from honey, pollen, and vegetable powders. The advertisements were categorical: "The pigments are implanted by hand by the beautician in a natural and therefore infallible procedure."

"If you want to change color and become light-skinned, it's easy: an implantation — and that's that!" trumpeted the governmental press. Alas! That wasn't that, at all.

In the end, the supreme authority made a firm proposal to native-born Dominicans: curdled milk, mayonnaise, copper, peach, honey, or tar — whatever the color, from then on they would powder themselves with wheat flour! It was done. And well done!

Thus did the people walk around in their skins. Thus did Trujillo's racism turn joyous Dominicans, for a long time, into ghosts.

Meanwhile, at the front end of the island, the drums were beating in the Republic of Haiti. The government was cultivating a taste for revelry in the masses. National holidays, patriotic festivals, parish feasts were turning into bacchanals. The coarse white rum called *clairin* flowed freely on every occasion. In marketplaces, public squares, parks, restaurants, schools, hospitals, and churches, officials ladled out "President Vincent's pepper-pot," a mixture of vegetables, tripe, what-have-you, garnished with political speeches slathered in thick sauces of nationalist demagogy. Public dances and private parties gathered bodies together for the next demographic explosions. To exotic rhythms, new dance steps were created, rather like the rotations of a hand drill. Whenever a government minister, a senator of the republic, a deputy of the people, a personnel director, or an office manager got married, grotesque carnival bands would take to the streets: the cobblestones of the capital shook beneath the tread of oxen painted half yellow, half green; spangled Indians wearing horns and feathers bent their bows; Africans showed off their monumental scarlet gums; polychrome butterflies with creaking wings frisked about among nurses and *papalois*; hieratic Hindus in white silk turbans passed solemnly by; huge grinning or frowning papier-mâché heads representing various big shots in Port-au-Prince danced along, keeping time to the music.

The drums were beating.

Games of chance — lotto, roulette, the lottery — filled the nights of adults and children alike. Rainy days were declared holidays.

The nation played, pranced, seethed with delight. Captivated by the carousal, drunkenness, and lechery served up by the Vincent administration, the Haitian people underestimated the menace of Trujillo.

—15—

A hand alights on Pedro Brito's arm. A cold, trembling hand. Like Adèle's, when she saw the thing churning up the sky over Elías Piña. It's the hand of the young woman whose cracked voice is still repeating: "*Perejil* . . ." The *l* has sucked up the *i*. The *e* has kicked out the *r*. The word has stuck in her throat. The young woman coughs; a faint scent of roses falls and shatters. Pedro repeats patiently: "*Perejil.*" She coughs again. The word is about to commit outright murder, all by itself. Pedro places his big callused hand over the cold hand of the unknown woman gripping his right arm and says, calmly: "*Perejil.*" The *negrita* murmurs: "*Perejil.*" The *p* bumps into the *l* someplace and the word goes head over heels. No doubt about it: another mouth that will prove completely useless and deserving of decapitation. "*¡Perejil!*" the *Guardia* will shout. Her *i* will telescope into the *j*. That's it! "*¡Mátalo! ¡Mátalo bien!*" the commandant will start yelling. "Kill her!"

The head will quickly know the astonishment of death.

A mess of a mouth!

Swallowed up by the night, Chicha Calma goes on her way, eyes front, her engine racket reinforced from time to time by the snoring of the passengers slumped on her rickety seats.

One man, probably a full-blown diabetic, is half-drenched in his own urine. Someone else mutters in his sleep about a girl he claims wheedled money out of him and skipped off to Curaçao to marry a Dutch fag with a mop of lavender hair . . . Chicha Calma puffs along. And a turkey hen that supposedly gobbled up a watch made of solid water . . . Chicha sways from side to side. And an American Negro sergeant rumored to have lost his penis to a knife one night in Trinidad during Carnival . . . Chicha gurgles. And a guitar people say played the mandolin like a cemetery . . . Chicha bursts out laughing. Swaying his head from side to side, a centenarian gentleman sits ruminating and spits up every twenty seconds, murmuring, "Sorry." A rooster tied somewhere on the luggage-rack tries out "Cock-a-doodle-doo," thinks better of it, and quietly swallows his pride. You can barely see the driver's head. It must still be thinking of its kilometers of kilometers. From Santiago to La Romana. Of asphalt. From Sánchez to Higüey. Of mud. From Monte Cristi to San Pedro. Of road metal. All through the country. Of bodies and songs. His Dominican bus-driver's head, lost in the darkness of the *guagua* among the passengers' tummy-rumblings and the barely perceptible voice of the young woman droning *"Perejil"* . . . The *j* has spat on the *i*. The word is in pain. If the workers demanded respect for their sweat, they might manage to beat back Trujillo's madness. In any case, Guillermo Sánchez is aware of the situation. Guillermo, *el trabajador,* the colossus with skin the color of mottled brick, and a cinnamon crew-cut. The workers had shouted: "*¡Maldita!* Speak out! Tell us what you think!"

There's no one like Guillermo Sánchez for talking to laborers and farmers in language they understand. His words always count, and go right to the point.

"*¡Coño!*" he'd shouted. "No one kills muscle-power!"

"Life needs it bad," a worker had piped up.

"The Dominican economy runs on Haitian sweat. You don't sabotage the machine that earns your living," Guillermo had continued.

"Sweat and sugar!" came the laconic cry.

"A compromise we'll have to live with," Guillermo Sánchez had wound up. "Until we organize ourselves for the victory of both peoples. Together, they can win!"

Pistons snorted, banged, throbbed, belched, spitting diesel oil ten meters in all directions, while belts creaked and raced impatiently. The workers bustled about with a gleam in their eyes. There is no possible comparison between Trujillo and the workers. He is the System, the kite-machine, the emblem-bird. They are the flesh the System chews into shreds. Oh, the sweat of honest labor, eternal and patient! He is the tunnel, they are the light at the end . . . The workers in the factory promised me to see the others, in Dajabón, Santiago, Ozama, Barahona: "*¡Compañeros! ¡Mañana temprano!* First thing tomorrow!" "*¡Seguro temprano!* Early, you bet!" Then the voices flew off over the cane fields. Voices that will go home to urge that the forces of labor come together to keep Haitian heads from rolling. At least, insofar as we can. The Organization is still just getting started.

Chicha slices through the black night air. In her carnage

she drags along the scent of wild daisies nodding by the roadside and scattered across the land as far as the eye can see. In its somber apparel, the Dominican night has a regal presence, crowned high overhead by a superb star. And to think that it's a Haitian star as well . . . Doubtless seen by everyone over there in Locaré, Boc-Banic, Ferrier, Maribaroux, Guayaba, Capotille, Ouanaminthe, by all the border people. By Adèle, my wife, whose caresses from last night I carry on my body: "You have danced inside me, belly to belly . . ." "And your heat has set me on fire!"

Pedro Alvarez Brito y Molina unclamps from his arm the clenched left hand of the young woman whose lips still struggle to whisper *"Perejil,"* even in her sleep. The *p* has done in the *r*. The word gets away from her. But it has not left her. It has besieged her. Subdued her. Colonized her. Resisting with her almost unconscious strength, she tries to tear herself free. She moans, babbles. Her voice betrays her terror at this unimaginable moment of life on the border and the deranged inhumanity now taking shape.

Suddenly she clutches Pedro. Offers him her perfume, says passionate things, speaks the name of a man: Roberto Gonzalez y Sabrini. Smiles. Comes. Stretches. Collapses, her lips shining with an uneasy happiness. She has not awakened. She is sleeping with the word. "Your body has wed mine," she breathes faintly through half-open lips. "But, oh! What wreckage is left?"

For the last forty-eight hours, the Haitian people of the border have been learning to say *"perejil."* A banal word. A kitchen herb. That can cost a life. If you can pronounce it well, you are Dominican, *blanco de la tierra,* and the soldiers present arms: "*¡Guardia, salud!*" But if the *r* wanders into the *i,* if the *j* absorbs the *l,* the *p* limps into the *r,* the *e* gets caught in the *j,* or if the *p,* the *l,* the *r* become dislocated, jam up, grab at one another, come undone, start scrapping, go off in a huff, then you are Haitian and ready for the firing squad: "*¡Guardia, fúsilelo!*"

"Your footsteps imprint their cadence in my body. I walk in the idea of you," sighs the young woman.

Chicha Calma abandons the road, plunging right into the daisy display and plowing through the short circuits of the lightning bugs. Chicha is scared. The wind from Elías Piña whispered in her ear just now.

"No one should dare to criticize the Guardia's mistake — a minor incident, a marginal massacre. And anyway, to make up for it, on the banks of that same Guayamuco River they have butchered four thousand seven hundred and eighty-four Haitian agricultural workers. Going on a trip? Travel on Panama Lines: you'll get there faster!"

The on-board wind-radio ferrets around, kicks up its heels, swerves, crackles: "Further reports of current statistics are expected momentarily."

Chicha pretends she hasn't heard. Basically, she cannot believe what she did just hear. Appalled, she strikes out boldly into the daisies, gets bogged down in their perfume, leaps over a plot of yucca. A cuckoo rolls its big dumb eyes, wide with fright. She cannot accept what she heard. She barely misses a cow snoozing under a fig tree. Cannot accept the fact. Mooing trails after her. Chicha barrels across country. Grazes one, two, three animal pens. Toward the far horizon. To escape. Escape what?

The wind-radio continues:

"The news is increasingly reassuring."

A sleeping child snores (time off for his guardian angel).

"There have been no moves by hostile forces, except for a few Dominican hotheads, some workers . . . And a few Haitian peasants have tried to resist! They have quickly been brought to heel, and enjoined not to obstruct the ongoing operation. In any case, there has never been any question of the lower classes dictating to the leading lights of the nation . . ."

Chicha groans with all her wood and metal. Chicha stamps and tramples. Sideswipes a chicken coop. The night crackles, cheeps, squawks. Chicha grumbles. She trashes the planks fencing a vegetable garden. The earth wakes up, drifts, wanders about. Chicha is fuming. No, definitely, she simply can't bring herself to accept the situation!

The wind comes back:

"Regarding the *cabezas* affair, Port-au-Prince is remaining studiously silent. Citizens are going about their business. Government offices are functioning normally. President Vincent has enough to eat."

It's understandable.

"So do his mistresses."

Perfectly comprehensible.

"So do their gigolos."

Only natural.

“So do even the dogs of the National Palace, whose barking curved the saber of the Emperor Jacques I. Be that as it may, Dominican troops and their officers, trained by American marines, are massed on the border and prepared to invade Haitian territory. Tonight at 6:30 at the National Cinema: the French drama *Ramuntcho,* with Louis Jouvet. Enjoy the show, dear listeners.”

Then the on-board radio attacks a Mozart allegro.

Beside herself, Chicha charges a hut, tramples some chick pea beds, goes around in circles, spews smoke, backfires. A burst of machine-gun bullets somewhere nails a life. Time, disturbed, opens one eye. Slinks off, aghast. Chicha wriggles, fulminates, explodes. *¡Calma!* Señorita Chicha! Calm down! You carry on your tires the spirit of the border people. A people who know how to ring changes on dissimulation, grasp nuances, dissect the parts of a whole, pin down rough estimates, fall back on stand-bys. A people living with the imponderable, facing sunshine and storms with equanimity. Quiet! Chicha! Calm down, please! You’re right, Don Pipo, my esteemed driver: I, Chicha, the *guagua* of the great markets of Maribaroux, Jimaní, Cerca, Los Posos — why am I losing my head, when I should be keeping it firmly on my springs? I’m flying off the handle! *¿Qué es eso?* What’s the matter with me! Incidentally, you crazy old Chicha *loca,* that damned temper of yours, it’s in your blood, the exuberant blood of the *hidalgos.* But still, Don Pipo, I overdo it. I’m afraid so, Chicha! We’ve been lugging our people here and there around the two lands for more than twenty years now.

We've seen them dance in Fort-Liberté. What rejoicing! Fireworks, lights everywhere. Get drunk in Monte Cristi. What a blowout! Wild music, hips in a whirl. Make wishes for good luck at the sulfur pond of Cerca-La-Source: handing around fighting cocks, fruit, straw hats, fried snacks, musical instruments, beribboned bottles. We've seen them haggling in Saint-Michel:

"Pork — three gourdes thirty centimes the slice. Just look at that piece."

"Three gourdes, no more."

"No, dearie, that's not the price, pigs are scarce these days."

"There are chickens aplenty. They're fresher and cheaper."

"It's just that I've come a long way, from Marmelade. The taxes, transportation, all that . . . Let's say three gourdes twenty centimes."

"Three gourdes, that's my price. And a good one!"

"I'll let you have the piece, so add a little something. Look how fat it is! Have a heart."

"I've got three gourdes."

"Three gourdes fifteen centimes, and we're done. Take it."

"Three."

"Three fifteen.

"Three."

"You're taking advantage of me."

"Three."

"I give up! It's yours."

It's always like that during the stops, Don Pipo, even during trips! True, Chicha! We've seen them laugh in Belladère, when both presidents met there with blaring music, lies, and blah-blah-blah: "Our two peoples have hard heads, clear consciences, and ravenous appetites," one of them babbled. Lament and complain in Banica: "The sky has turned off the water." We've seen our folks mingle and blend together in Ouanaminthe, where the feast of the Assumption is a festival for the whole border. Strangers embrace, and without asking permission, too! Remember, Chicha? Wonderful! Really fantastic! "*¡Buenos días amigos!*" "*¿Y qué?*" "*¿Cómo le va?*" Like celebrating the end of a war. With flowers, cars, brass bands, flags, carillons, firecrackers, drums, balloons, toys. People going back and forth, from both sides. The border guards waving away passports. All hard feelings are forgotten. And what great clients! Wow! *Muchachitas* and *muchachitos* melting into one another on your seats, Chicha! Just thinking about it makes my chassis tingle, Don Pipo! And such exciting goods! Without any surliness or petty hassles from the border guards. *Free port* all along the border: macaroni from Santo Domingo; kerosene from Port-au-Prince; shoes from Santiago de los Caballeros; Havanas from Cuba; trousers from Lascahobas; salt beef from Gonaïves; mattresses from Dajabón; butter from Saint-Marc; soap from Puerto Plata; dried fish from Le Borgne; aluminum tumblers from Puerto Rico; milk from the Cibao Valley; duty-free French perfumes from Martinique; chairs from Gros-Morne; underwear from Curaçao; lard from Monte Cristi; caps *made in Jamaica*; wicker baskets from Mancenille; tinned chicken from Trinidad;

granulated brown sugar from Macorís; *clairin* from Thomonde — and watch out with that last item! The gentlemen head off for a good cocktail: strong white rum, a twist of lime, and mouths start to gape and explode! Your heart just gets happy. Ahem — Don Pipo! Most of the time, our people have coffee or cocoa in Los Posos. And then those jokers always piss on my tires. Which really stings! What do you expect, old girl? They're customers. Ah, yes! I've certainly hauled my clunker carcass around, on asphalt, beaten earth, over rocky ground and underbrush. And I've hauled your head around as well, Don Papito Consuelo Pipo y Gonzalez, driver of mine! Oh, yes, I've lugged your baby face around. From La Romana to Monte Cristi. With its smallpox scars. From Sánchez to Higüey. Over mud. Across ruts. And I've spread rumors, too. A whole bunch. From the border region. Nasty gossip, Chicha. Hmm! Between the two of us, it was... it was... it was swell. Remember, it was in Cerca-La-Source. At the feast. Of Saint Agnes. Or Saint Nicholas. Or else at... Come on, now, old girl! We can't expect to remember clearly anymore! We've celebrated so many saints' days, Chicha: Saint-Ferdinand in Monte Cristi, Saint Peter in Terrier Rouge, Saint James in Santiago de los Caballeros, Saint Suzanne in Sainte Suzanne, Altagracia in Higüey, Saint Martin in Dondon. We're getting old, Señora Chicha; our faculties are dwindling, failing! The people would arrive in a crowd, fan out over the small pink square right across from the indigo chapel with the puce steeple. I remember well, Don Papito Consuelo Pipo y Gonzalez, my sozzled driver! Watch it —

no back talk, Chicha, you jalopy! I remember too, just imagine. They weren't shy at all about unrolling their straw mats in the walkways of the public square to take naps, and jam up traffic. I mean foot traffic, of course, because you, you were stashed, stowed, parked, abandoned somewhere. By Don Papito Consuelo y Gonzalez, my maniac driver! I admit that, Chicha: I am a maniac, but the machine has to step aside every once in a while. The passengers didn't complain about the inconvenience. Abandoned by my ridiculous *borracho* of a driver! *¡Miserere!* When I drink, you lose your pedals, Chicha, my bird-brain! But Pipo! I saw them too, the people! They would mill around, elbowing one another, like crazy ants, streaming up and down the main street of the little town. Ah, Pipo! We always wind up coming back to that sorry mess of ruts — you couldn't go even forty kilometers an hour on it. *¡Está bien!* That's enough! Rein in that murderous imp of an imagination, Chicha *loca!* That muddy, narrow, pot-holed mess. No way around it. In spite of every detour and maneuver. Always the end of the line. Throngs of people, jampacked, crowding into the street. Trampling, jostling, yelling. Then laughing. Slapping one another on the back. It would seem as if the entire population of Cerca had swarmed out into the street, wouldn't it, you miserable *guagua?* It was in the midst of one such show of human warmth that I first saw *el señor* Pedro and *la señora* Adèle. Such a handsome couple! Like a brand-new pair of klaxons! They seemed to possess the whole of life. They were necking, smooching, he in a vanilla suit with a brown windowpane check, she in a flowing dress of white silk with dainty olive-green polka dots. They were saying things to each other, Chicha, such things! Ah, yes, Chicha, such things:

"You're still courting me, Pedro, as in Thomassique."

"Or Maribaroux!"

"We are the lovers of the border."

"We have eyes for two skies."

"A shiver for two breezes."

"Wings for two winds."

"A kiss for two countries."

"Oh, no! On that point, I'm selfish, Adèle."

Their laughter clung to people and objects like a magic trick.

"I'm yours, completely yours, my jealous one, Pedrito *celoso!*"

A combo of three slender mustachioed Dominicans (a banjo wearing white, a maraca all in gold, and a trumpet in a black suit with green trim, a cream vest, and a red bow tie) had crossed the border freely, and their merengues electrified the now pickled pilgrims. Don Pedro, *un poco borracho,* slipped a rolled-up yellow bandana around Señora Adèle's waist and held the two ends, one in each hand, while the young lady clasped her perfumed fingers sensually behind his neck and kept it warm. They twirled in the fire of their hips, he clicking his tongue and stamping his feet, she dizzily lighting up the night with her bright smile, ready to take flight — they were so light they seemed made of nothing. A marvel to see. They throbbed with ecstatic joie de vivre.

They drew close, pushed away, clung together, reared back, a tantalizing torture that left your throat dry and your temples pounding.

"Do they dance like this in Cuba, Pedro?"

"Here, on your side or mine, it's the merengue, or close enough. In Cuba, it's the rumba. In Jamaica, Trinidad, the English islands, it's calypso."

"The rhythms are all alike!"

"And in Martinique, Guadeloupe, the French islands in general, it's the beguine."

"Show-off!"

"You made me miss a step. People are watching us, Douce Folie."

"*Gallo,* crow away!"

"The Caribbean speaks through dancing."

"I disagree, *señor*. Everyone dances."

"It's not the same — we're born with the dances, the chain dances or contredanses, because we are the crucible of joys and sorrows."

"No politics, Monsieur Brito — you've missed another step. Et *la gente te mira!* They're looking at you! Pay attention, *macho!*"

The candles burning on the front doorsteps of the village leaped and swayed to keep up with the dancers. The rolled-up yellow bandana rubbed the waist of the doña, who undulated, floated, whirled, while Don Pedro — head back, eyes closed, lips parted, his Adam's apple sliding up and down — abandoned himself to a kind of bliss:

"¡Dame, dámelo bien, mujer mía!"
"¡Toma, tómalo bien, hombre mío!"
"¡Yo vivo, coño! ¡Me siento bien!"
*"¡Igual, mi amor! ¡Cómo tú!"**

They were twining around each other like that when a sergeant and two soldiers suddenly seized *el señor* Pedro Alvarez Brito y Molina. As the yellow bandana slipped from the waist of Doña Adèle to lie unfurled on the ground, the soldiers dragged their prisoner to a police station the color of curdled milk. The crowd fell abruptly silent, the Dominican combo melted away: the spirit had gone out of the festival at Cerca-La-Source like a flame that had run out of wick. The straw mats folded up all by themselves. The crowd vanished down side streets, engulfed by the night. Me, Chicha, I was shaking where I stood, shaking in my bolts, my rods, my springs. Ah-ha, you fraidy-cat, you can say that again! And when the bell of the indigo chapel tolled limply in its steeple, there came in counterpoint the sound of a broken heart, as if Cerca-La-Source were hurting all over. It was the *señora* crying, Don Pipo! . . . Hey there, Mamzelle Chicha, no extravagance, if you please. First you bite back at words you can't really figure out (words written on the wind), and now you're going all misty over memories of your jaunts to Neiba, Val-

---

* "Give it to me, really give it to me, woman of mine!"
"Take it, really take it, man of mine!"
"Damn, I'm alive! I feel wonderful!"
"Me too, my love! Just like you!"

lières, Barranca, and I don't know where! You're dithering when you should be hurrying along. Come on, Chicha Calma, you old tin can! You're just rambling. Let's wake up. Start using your head. Our passengers are getting impatient. Oh, really, you windbag driver! So I'm the one who was talking? That's rich!

"She's right," Don Pipo told himself. "It all comes from me — even her reproach is me talking. What do you expect? You have to have someone else — to give the impression of a reply! Especially when you're driving along with faces like these in the *guagua*. Drained. Exhausted. Frightened."

The *guagua* coughs. Bumps. *¡Cuidado, compadre!* The driver shakes himself, rubs his eyes.

Puffing, popping, rasping, Chicha breaks the spell of the daisies and with a thousand little moves, maneuvers her way back to her kilometers of asphalt. *¡Bueno!* Of mud. Of underbrush. Of rocky road. *¡Bueno!* The air she tunnels and barrels through moans like Adèle's mouth when she tries to pronounce the word.

And yet, it's not so difficult. *¡Mira Adèle!* The Yaque River rolls the word downstream, the Sierra de Neiba rustles it through trees, the Bahoruco broods it, the Cibao gallops it over the horizon, and I who have known and explored your body, making your breasts blossom in spite of your womb's reluctance to bear my fruit, I, *tu marido de dos años,* I pronounce it, I say the word, without smudges, correctly: "*Perejil.*"

"This word will kill you, Adèle. Practice it."

"What you should say is, 'Men, in their stupidity, will kill you, Adèle.' Because in my own language, when my head's in the right place, I say the word: *Persil! Persil! Persil! Du persil pour ma couronne! Du persil pour mon royaume! Mon cheval! Mon cheval, pour du persil!** Without a hitch. Or hesitation. Flawlessly. *Sí señor,* I say the word, in my own language."

"Don't get upset, Adèle. Take your sedative. It's time. Don't forget what Juan said."

"I'm not upset. I say *'perejil'* for your people. *'Persil'* for mine. *Voilà, m'sieur! 'Sociedad'* for your people, *'société'* for mine. *'La muerte'* for yours, *'la mort'* for mine. *'God'* for another. *'Dios'* for you. *'Dieu'* for me. *Voilà, m'sieur!*"

"Actually, there is only one common language: love."

"And don't forget hatred, too!"

"People are so hard to put in words."

"Hand me that sedative, please, Pedro."

"How lovely she was that evening!" thinks Pedro. "Fragile and lovely in her distractions and bewilderments."

The wind from Elías Piña whispers:

"In the end, they were unable to spare the children, or the women, or the elderly. Still, they could have, if the Haitian authorities had asked them to . . . We can't be more considerate than the Haitian government itself, after all. This just in: Hitler presses his claim on the Danzig Corridor."

The on-board-wind-radio-town-crier is quiet for a mo-

---

* Parsley! Parsley! Parsley! My crown for some parsley! My kingdom for some parsley! My horse! My horse! My horse, for some parsley!

ment before continuing, with Debussy's "Clair de Lune" in the background:

"We were also unable to spare the disabled and infirm . . . No Red Cross agency anywhere in the world spoke up on their behalf."

Chicha Calma gives a start, but turns a deaf ear.

"Nor did any other international, philanthropic, humanitarian organization . . ."

—16—

In the wee hours of the night, in his palace where rumors from the capital, snatches of music, distant train whistles, sirens, and factory racket came to die, the Caudillo would think about the Citadel. Sometimes he placed it in the heart of Santo Domingo, among the pigeons and flower sellers, and sometimes on the banks of the Ozama, with the fishermen and redfish, or else he saw it in the half-light of the main thoroughfares, with their streetwalkers and melancholy. He treated it as a plaything, tossed it up to the stars, caught it in his arms, showed it off to crowds, took it on a triumphant tour of the city, visiting the churches, union halls, museums, hospitals, cafés, fondling it, dandling it. It was his daughter, his knout, his dog, his foot-soldier, his wife, his apotheosis. What a weapon he would have made of it! *What* a weapon!

The Caudillo simply could not understand why that fearsome and fantastic thing-near-the-sky was not Dominican.

To shake off his sadness, he sent, as usual, for poets in the naive folk tradition, and had them gather in the palace courtyard. Their different local customs and native costumes presented striking contrasts, while their vibrant voices revealed their varying ethnic backgrounds, so that the group gave the impression of a shimmering and sonorous mosaic. All these men, however, had one thing in common: heartfelt passion. This pleased the dictator, who without further ado gave the order to delve into the nation's folk memory.

Wearing a lilac overcoat, his eyes hidden beneath a wide-brimmed hat of woven palm fronds, a wizened old man the color of macaroni stepped up and began to speak.

Oyez! The poet:

"The Haitian general Jean-Pierre Boyer reunited the East and the West. The same sun rose and set on the country, the same perfumes floated out over the night landscapes, the same voices struck up the work songs, the women gave birth to the same wails of life."

The Generalissimo made a vague gesture that the storyteller must have interpreted in a split second, since the tone of his recital changed abruptly.

Oyez! The poet tries again:

"But this union had lasted too long. And the East separated from the West. The Dominican sun rose more promptly, and work sang more melodiously in our fields."

A certain smile hovered around the ultra-pale face of Rafael Leónidas Trujillo y Molina. As if the boss were digesting a particularly toothsome meal.

The elderly folk poet stopped, pulled a bottle from the right-hand pocket of his lilac overcoat, drained it in one go, spat, hummed a local tune, then wandered silently off to the left of the crowd of storytellers.

Another poet, quite young, swarthy and half naked, lay

prostrate before the Caudillo and declaimed.

Oyez! The young troubadour:

"Pedro Santana, the Dominican president, wanted to hitch the nation to the Yankees' star. The fires of Capotillo set Santana's dream ablaze."[17]

The boss stopped him right there.

The audience of khaki-clad soldiers and lackeys in white aprons was surprised to see Trujillo take over as director and assign various roles himself, lining up the poets to have them parade by in a certain order.

First storyteller (medium height; flat, yellow, freckled face):

"France and Spain were determined to support us without any difficulties

"Provided they could gobble up Dominican beef whenever they pleased."

Second storyteller (short, bald, tanned):

"To get his hands on Samaná Bay

"Uncle Sam was ready to do anything.

"He offered our companies *half and half:*

"gross income split right down the middle."

Third storyteller (shining apple cheeks, top hat):

"Our presidents Báez and Heureaux

"tried to sell us to America.

"Providence saved us."

Fourth storyteller (black, with a tender and ardent gleam in his eye):

"One of these days, we really must

"change our style to: *No tickee, no washee!*"

Fifth storyteller (broad back, round shoulders, heavy legs, light complexion):

"Now we want a country shaped by

"agriculture,

"hydraulic engineering,

"roads, and harbors."

Sixth storyteller (white, double chin, ample derrière):

"We want a people who are

"well-fed, healthy,

"clothed, housed, educated."

Trujillo abruptly dismissed the poets and sent urgently for his Minister of the Interior, with whom he spent the whole night closeted in his office drawing up a wish-list of . . . weapons.

The first rays of the sun were just gilding the steep banks of the Ozama when the President and his Minister read through the order one last time:

70,100 bougainvillea-firing machine guns

13,250 iron cannons

4,316 cistern-gurgle guns

400 copper cannons

271 sulfurous-water faucets

6,613 homing grenades

10,014 bayonets

5,500 hoarse pistols

600 dragon-blazoned cast-iron cannons

7,000 cavalry sabers with sheaths and hilts of gilded copper, with various decorations.

All kinds of artillery shells, unspecified, to be selected by the contractor.

The President then ordered the Minister of the Interior to add to the list — if only for form's sake — the Citadel. "Our neighbors," he said, "must hear our voice. We haven't yelled loud enough to terrify them." *(Top Secret.)*

Hitting two birds with one stone, the President now ordered:

8,000 smugglers from Spain
6,450 counterfeiters from Lebanon
3,714 vagrants from Palestine
1,215 hired assassins from Jordan
467 pederasts from Germany
265 predators from Greece,

to be inserted between the thighs of the Dominican female population to whiten the nation. The President expressed the wish that during the operation, Dominican women would prove very tender, gentle, and accommodating toward the aforementioned, so as to facilitate their own fertility for breeding purposes.

The Caudillo asked for a glass of milk, into which he dropped two cubes of white sugar. And lost his temper. As the sun rose, all of life seemed bitter to him. He ordered that a one-hundred-and-twenty-one gun salute be fired right in the courtyard of the palace, and he counted the shots angelically. Then he drank his milk. Closed his eyes.

And did not dream of the Citadel.

—17—

"Even religions aren't giving a thought to the Haitian border people. Cutex, ladies, for lovely hands!"

The on-board-wind-radio frisks off, mischievously carrying Debussy's "Clair de Lune" away into the night.

The *negrita* is still clamped to his arm, there's nothing Pedro can do about that, and he vomits the word into her ear. The young woman tries again. So does Brito. And so does the young woman. The *l* has skidded into the *r*. The driver's head — which has been eating up the kilometers on the road from the sugar factory to Elías Piña for a while now — brakes hard. In a stink of burning rubber the *guagua*'s wheels screech to a halt. A flight of wood pigeons seems to have gone astray in the darkness, stirring awake the scent of plum trees. The middle-aged man fills his pipe. The passengers get off to stretch their legs. In the distance, *una bachata* mourns in despair. A star deserts its regiment. The song is wounding itself more and more cruelly, while a voice weeps steadily inside the *guagua*. The Dominican night is like a corpse in a coffin, and this feeling of life stopped short has lasted a good few minutes. The song begins again, haunting, oppressive. The middle-aged man has not relighted his pipe but kept it tucked stiffly into the corner of his mouth. Like a sentinel.

You are a thorn inside me.
Each move we make
Drives it in deeper,
Reviving the pain:
We are trapped by love!

wails the *bachata.*

A soul flits by, as silky as gossamer. The song is sent under the yoke. Then strangled. Locusts rake the night with monotonous parallel notes. A passenger, his whole body trembling, brays, "*¡La muerte!*"

The *negrita* falls forward. The word has killed her. Through her throat. Uvula. Tongue. Teeth. Lips. Through her breath. Given the circumstances, one wonders if the Devil hasn't joined Trujillo's Cabinet.

"We'll take her body to Cerca-Cabajal," murmurs the man with the pipe. "That's where she comes from."

Her heart, however, had blossomed in Ciudad Trujillo, the capital, in the house of the young engineer Roberto Gonzalez y Sabrini, *su marido de cuatro años.* An elusive scent of roses drifts around the *guagua.* How many lives of these two peoples have become entwined behind the scenes!

The on-board radio pipes up flippantly:

"No heads worth stuffing — the international museums claim these heads have no personality. They lack freshness, warmth, vitality. They provoke no artistic curiosity. They cannot, in any way, provide a feast for the eyes. So, the heads are wandering around on their own, of no interest to anybody. (Pause.) So there goes a good business opportunity for both governments, right down the drain. Brugard, the best rum in the country, brings you the time: exactly 3:47 in the morning."

On the night of his arrest in Cerca-La-Source, Pedro Brito was accused of activism and thrown into prison. The poor *señora* couldn't sleep for three months.

Chicha shudders.

"Clair de Lune" dissolves completely into the darkness.

"We're not far from Elías Piña," says the driver. "We'd better prepare ourselves."

"The Dominican nation has never been in such good health," announces a firm voice.

The voice promptly guggles. There is the sound of a body falling into the grass beside the road. Glowworms flare up.

"All taken care of?" asks the man with the pipe.

"*¡Pronto, señor!*" comes the reply.

"*¡Está bien! ¡Está bien!*"

The voice had belonged to an agent of the *Cabezas Haitianas* Committee — the CHC — on duty in the *guagua*, with instructions to find out what the Dominican people think of the massacre. Well, he found out.

"*Compañeros,* listen to me," exclaims Pedro Brito fervently, but a passenger interrupts him.

"It's a bloodbath."

"Precisely," agrees Pedro Brito.

The driver, relieving his bladder on the *guagua*'s right front tire, cuts the discussion short.

"You know this as well as I do: it's all because of that word."

–18–

Ever since the sky over Elías Piña dribbled into the clutches of the raptor-kite, the Dominican people of both lands have been teaching the Haitian people of both lands the proper pronunciation of "*perejil*." This word has never before known such notoriety or roused such strong emotions. Fefa Rodriguez of Dajabón nailed it to the lips of Pierre Charmant of Vallières. César Gómez of Jimaní nestled it between the breasts of Rose Antoine of Boucan-Bois. Between two glasses of Bermudez rum, Julian Nuñez y Jiménez hefted, handled, and gargled it for his friend Serge Laplanche, a teacher in Cerca-La-Source. Two peoples, to say one word, with kisses, hopes, dance steps, glances, sighs, fears, gifts, complicities, understandings, and exhilarating joys.

In Malpasse and Malpaso, on both sides of the border, along kilometers of paths across mountains and plains, through swamps and forests, all day long in endless procession, folks young and old bear on their heads large white rocks that they set down on the ground to sit on, face to face, looking silently into one another's eyes.

A voice, in the almost uncanny head tones of a skeletal man with chocolate skin, chants: "*¡Perejil!*" The word rises immediately from thousands of Haitian and Dominican throats, like a slow, thick, heavy incantation, then subsides, sucked into an immense air pocket, only to sail out over the heads of the chanters on the white rocks before collapsing once more into an indistinct slurry. A word that has flashed fire from eyes and made blood boil, crossed rivers and galloped over plains, but cannot emerge unscathed from Haitian lips. A death-dealing word: "*¡Perejil!*" A humble pot herb from a kitchen garden.

The Dominican whose voice fills kilometers of paths across mountains and plains, through swamps and forests, is blind in one eye.

One blustery night, people say, a moth put out his right eye, so the warmth of his body sought refuge in the other eye and in his extraordinary voice. He has just spent more than fifty hours teaching the word, which, ill at ease on Haitian lips, has declared itself unsuited to them.

In the end, the man with the chocolate skin breaks down, his other eye blinded, this time by his own gaze: "I've seen so much that things attack me as if I were Abel to their Cain. I die a victim of this cruel vision. Remember that whenever anyone points a gun at anything — at the song of a child, for example."

Those were his last words.

In Pedernales, hundreds of Dominican men and women with jugs of honey and sweet melon juice spend their days doling out the mixture to hundreds of Haitians of both sexes and all ages.

Lips touched by this drink soften, grow more flexible, and according to village elders, will be able to pronounce the word with ease. Each Dominican jug on a Haitian lip releases a whispering like a kiss, so that Pedernales is wreathed in a murmur as dense as the rumble of a popular uprising.

But the word, intoxicated by too much eroticism, has been damaged. A word gleaned from the canebrakes, breathed in the concupiscence of lovers clasped in each other's arms, a word grown in the fields, taken up and passed around by hands, throats, sexes: a word making the most of compromise, willing to be both a rallying cry and the ramp to a slaughterhouse. A word that both peoples of both lands strive desperately to say well so that one people may not be the other's guilty conscience, but the blazing hearth of their home.

Two black children, a girl of five and a boy of four, met entirely by chance one midday at the foot of a lemon tree growing on the border itself, not far from Hinche.

They were born in Bahoruco, he to the Haitian François family, and she to the Dominican Cortez family. They fell easily into friendship, as children usually do.

And here they are, amusing themselves by casually hopping on one foot from this side of the border to the other, and back: now on Haitian territory, now on Dominican soil. Their laughter pokes holes of youthful freshness in the landscape. The game has been going on for more than an hour.

So here it is: the little girl asks the little boy to please say "*perejil.*" Nathan — that's the boy's name — opens his mouth. The word has seized up. Nathan, all smiles, tells

Juanita — that's the girl's name — that he just can't say *"perejil."* Juanita ceremoniously takes Nathan's hand. The two children go off to sit under the lemon tree. The little Dominican girl has the little Haitian boy rehearse the word.

The day is waning, and the children are still sing-songing *"¡Perejil! ¡Perejil!"* A light breeze wafts their voices, their prattle, their bravos, their wonderment away into the distance. A locust stipples the twilight. The first clumps of stars come out. Then Nathan and Juanita fall asleep side by side.

They'll be found the next morning, at first light, holding hands around a bouquet of parsley. The border guards won't have the courage to cut off either head.

The lemon tree will have burst completely into bloom.

A bell rings. No one can tell whether it's from here or the next hamlet over. The people in both villages simply wind up their watches at the same time.

"The day is young, *compañero!"*

"Then it's a good day to plant."

"And to love one another!"

"With God's help."

It seems that Atilo Francisco Manuel y Pérez, the popular merchant from Jimaní, can no longer sell his wares in Fond-Parisien. The border guards are getting meaner and keep turning him back. Crossing the border is strictly forbidden. "Indisputable" (as usual) "and serious reasons of State" (this time around), announces a notice from the CHC with bell, drum, and trumpet on every street corner of the towns and villages, the posts and the outposts along the Dominican border.

It's really too bad, because of all the vendors of the border region, no one beats Atilo Francisco for bargains: with him, a pound of raw sugar at 15 centimes falls to 2 centimes; a chuck end of beef at 20 centimes is only 15 with Atilo; the price of cod goes from 60 to 25 centimes; a case of vermicelli at 3 gourdes is 1.85 gourdes; trousers of broadcloth cost 2.75 gourdes, while other dealers won't take 3.50 gourdes. Lately, at the market in Fort-Liberté, where iron rat traps were selling at 3.25 gourdes the dozen, you could buy them from Francisco Atilo for 2.10 gourdes. Children's wool-knit booties, men's leather and patent-leather shoes, women's shoes in fine colored calfskin, silk, morocco, with spangles or embroidery — all can be found among Atilo's goods at half price.

From now on, the vendors will have to take the smugglers' routes to get to the rural markets. Because it has been decided that the Dominican border will be opened only when the Haitian population can properly pronounce the word "*perejil*."

For the same reason, the clock in Dajabón has been put out of order and no longer tells time for the schoolchildren of Ouanaminthe. The Dominican police sergeant in Banica may no longer savor the *clairin* of Mont-Organisé, nor the priest of Elías Piña buy his eggs in Belladère, nor the surveyor of Ferrier measure ground where he pleases.

"Indisputable, irreversible, serious reasons of State": that's the message from the *Cabezas Haitianas* Committee.

And now Juan Pablo's big old rooster is trying to pick a

fight with Pierre Gauthier's Cochin-China cock. They'll sort it all out; they've been *compañeros* for the past three months now, in all the *gaguerres.*

A bee spirals through the air, a flighty dot of gold — it must be a queen. A mass of brown wings follows her, streaking through the sunshine and the azure sky. En route! Time to tackle the Dominican fields.

If your soup steams, my mouth waters. You call your children, I hear their footsteps and think of mine. When you weed your garden, I breathe the joy of your land.

"You led me to a country of tall trees, *amigo!*"

"I showed you a country where the birds soar on mighty wings, *amigo!*"

Urbain and Prospero are neighbors who have become fast friends. When one belches, the other says " 'Scuse me." They share more or less the same interests and are both — among other things — tireless revelers who show up at any celebration within a hundred leagues of the border: a dance at Duverger, a blowout at Cercado, *raras*[18] and drum-thumping festivities at Trois-Bois-Pins, a banquet at Ranquitte, a party at Las Matas, a fair at Victorine, a wedding at San José de Ocoa, cockfights at Cabeza-Cachón — wherever drums beat, drink flows, and girls chatter.

Urbain is a blob of gleaming black fat. He has a huge head as round and smooth as a cue ball sitting directly atop sloping shoulders, a jelly-belly that far outranks his chest, no teeth, a jolly laugh, and a plump pair of varicose-veined bowlegs underpinning the entire ensemble. According to his godmother, a centenarian Dominican lady with amber skin, he was born in Dame-Jeanne-Cassée,* a border post maintained by the Republic of Haiti in the *arrondissement* of Lascahobas. Urbain can't swear to that himself, however; all he knows is that he grew up somewhere between the two lands and now lives in Miguel, on the outskirts of Cercado-Cercado, in the Dominican district of Las Matas (Neiba).

Prospero is a tall fellow the color of terra cotta. His right eye stares straight ahead, as if on guard duty, while the left one can't stay still. No one can say what disjointed motion propels Prospero forward, but defying all the laws of gravity, he never falls. He usually wears an expression of childlike glee. Born in Dajabón, he still cannot explain his presence in Cercado, where he in fact possesses a whole third of a hectare of good soil.

Urbain and Prospero cultivate their gardens together without worrying whether the corn ripens in Haitian territory or the potatoes flourish in the Dominican Republic. They care only about welcoming the burgeoning green shoots and cradling the fruits of their labors in their hands. Their four wives — Joséphine, Esperancia, Julie, Amanda — are devoted to them. Their twenty-eight children (thirteen girls, fifteen boys) play in the same courtyard, eat and sleep beneath the same long bamboo bower covered with fragrant vetiver. Not one of them knows for sure whether Urbain or

---

* Broken Demijohn, or Broken Rum Jug.

Prospero is his or her father, and besides, the two bosom friends couldn't care less, as long as the kids have food on the table and clothes on their backs.

If Urbain and Prospero ever happen to quarrel, it's just for a change, to pass the time, tease one another, or forget some petty annoyance. Their spats always dissolve in hearty back-slapping and little glasses of orange-peel wine in Doña Rosita Manuel's neighborhood shop, a ritual that leaves fat Urbain waddling and Prospero tilting dangerously off-center.

Lately, though, they haven't been speaking. They're keeping their distance. It has come to their attention that by order of Ciudad Trujillo, with the agreement of Port-au-Prince, death will soon come to sit down between them, and they are growing desperately sad.

"The worms in your corpse will eat me up, too, amigo!"

Never in living memory have the border communities seen such a gathering of people, from Mancenille opposite Monte Cristi to Anses-à-Pitre near Las Damas: a vast area of mountains, flowers, insects, rivers and streams, rodents, plains, birds, containing more than a hundred thousand souls, Dominicans and Haitians, speaking to one another in a language that only they can understand — the language of the border, nourished by local customs, history, and the human heart.

Amid the tumult of voices, in the smell of sweat, across the solid sea of heads, they signal broadly to one another with hands, hats, branches, hankies, as if words, lacking enough strength, thrust, or memory, were just not coming to mind. Or had simply betrayed them.

Josefina Cabral is of one flesh with Robert Isidore; Alfredo Colón has weeded Valérie Jean-Pierre's garden. But words are floundering, jumping the tracks: the clearance has no conscience democracy has decreed without receptacle or contribution inflicted on the crystal chandeliers of the dry walls memory has no history of contact one can likewise try to maintain the capitals that have refused the instrument roofs the eyelids you see have no pretext as there is no river without its scholar of hieratic acquaintances for example in Ciudad Trujillo the guns listened to the bells of Saint-Anne's while remembering open cohesion therefore a daily paper with a homing device so they won't lose their rust proposes in mathematics: "Unknown and roughly estimated reasons of State." The roses have balked at the social benevolence of the penitentiary advances and the crosses hand over —

Words are *slavering!*

Talking drivel!

They have buckled, warped! They've covered their tracks, ignored the rules of their game. Men have driven them mad. And they're in the streets, those men: in Santiago de Los Caballeros, their paunches slung with cartridge belts; in Puerto Plata, brandishing signs emblazoned with the Jolly Roger; in Sabana, in battle dress — boots, overalls, stilettos, knives, daggers, with sticks of dynamite front and center. In San Pedro de Macorís, they're already at the table, savoring the aroma of their trophies:

"A head should know how to scream when you stab it."

"The bullet is the essential invention."

"Especially the noise."

"Without that, it makes less of an impression."

"The Generalissimo prescribes cold steel."

"When you get right down to it, your machete is more heroic."

With the patience, finesse, scruples, tics, know-how, and even the anguish of the true artist, the Dominican authorities methodically plan the genocide. How could you expect words to escape mutilation? It doesn't matter which one! *Perejil* or any other! The word "harvest" isn't promising; "kindness" lacks warmth; "liberty" has no resonance . . . The bird no longer builds its nest in the splendor of the day; man no longer conceives his plans in serenity of spirit or majesty of feeling. Words are out of joint. Candidates for orthopedics. Doctor's note: They left hope a shambles.

According to Don Agustín de Cortoba and the alcalde Preguntas Feliz, Haitian lips have massacred the word. There is nothing either constructive or cooperative about Haitian lips. They have abandoned the word. Deceived the word. Swindled it. Revenge is on the menu. Haitian lips will not carry the word off to heaven. They must pay — and richly! Without any kind of attenuating circumstances. Or grounds for appeal . . .

In the Dominican Republic, madness now reigns as supreme reason. "Reasons of State etc., etc." proclaims the *Cabezas Haitianas* Committee, approved and applauded by the House of Representatives, communal councils, and courts; praised and glorified by the armed forces of land and sea; congratulated and encouraged by the urban and rural police forces; honored and beatified by big business, industry, the central banks; tolerated and accepted by the diplomatic corps; supported and championed by the archdioceses, dioceses, Protestant sects, and fraternal organizations (the Brotherhood United in Faith of El Seibo, the Indissoluble Fraternity of Santo Domingo, the Perfect Union of Puerto Plata, the Philanthropy of Baní); but denounced by youth organizations, reviled by school districts, condemned by the Artists' Association, anathematized by trade guilds, rejected by labor unions, decried by the International Association for the Defense of Political Prisoners, vilified by agricultural cooperatives, resisted by peasant movements, and opposed with the utmost rigor by the people.

In this free-for-all of instincts and interests, what word would have emerged unscathed? And who wouldn't have doubts about the soundness of words? Let us pray.

The grand design of a national government is to kill people through the power of a word . . . The way we have pillaged, bombed, raped, burned in the name of the fatherland; mocked, cheated, stolen, murdered in the name of right and reason; pursued, tortured, imprisoned, banished in the name of liberty. The way we have hated in the name of charity, humiliated in the name of friendship, deceived in the name of goodness and religion. The way we have cuckolded tenderness and affection, disguised rascality as piety, backed slander in the face of decency, spread lawlessness instead of revolution, trampled honesty while rewarding fraud, presented sadism as humor, talked of moderation to the hungry, development to the illiterate, social harmony to the exploited, and peaceful coexistence to the poor. Let us pray.

Words have birth certificates — and death certificates, too. We have coupled joy with laughter, steeples with cloudless skies, awakening with sunshine, and work with eager hands. Throughout our great linguistic age, we have linked intelligence with light, youth with generosity, change with revolution, and hope with harvest time. We have found the highest physical expression of mankind in dance, and spiritual transcendence in love; we have built houses for protection, discovered medicines for health, worked the land for nourishment. And to guide the human mind we have words that express our needs: bread for hunger, culture for understanding, poetry for beauty. Words that translate our feelings: duty towards our country, the worship of God, the love of art. Just as we have created words for the shame of humanity: lies, envy, hatred, treachery, rape, tyranny. As a weapon against the border people, Rafael Leónidas Trujillo suggested "*perejil.*"

Ah, we human beings and our words, we know we are complex, changeable — and cruel!

Night has already fallen on the night of the world; our children will look no longer for their marbles gone astray in the tall grass . . .

Let us pray.

—19—

Chicha Calma gets underway again, heading for Elías Piña. Oof! And about time, too. The wind, it's like a good mechanic: doesn't lie. We're not making anything up, Chicha, that's what everyone says, Doña Chicha. So what, Don Drunken Driver! I remember when the dry little wind of La Vega slipped word to us, an hour beforehand, about the workers' strike in San Pedro. No sooner said than done: the Guardia charged the workers, the women, the children. They burned the banners, signs, and flags in the middle of the street, blacked out the slogans on the wall, kicked in the doors of houses. Heads rolled.

"Lucky Strike means fine tobacco! Can you beat that?"

And the on-board radio adopts a tone by turns brazen, curt, and grave, like the voice of Benito Mussolini. "Power is a gift from death, and I, I spin and cut the thread!"

Oh yes, Mamzelle Chicha, the wind-radio is an old snoop. It knows things, says things. But sometimes it gets on my nerves, Don Pipo! The Devil take that wind! *¡Está bien, Doña Chicha! ¡Está bien!* What the hell do we care if Don Pérez de Cortoba's wife goes on the rag three times a month? Aha, now you get me, you doddering wind-bag driver! You have no idea! And why should we believe that rivers go home every evening to the Milky Way? That spring peas are the breasts of girls who died young? That if the moon doesn't scoot out of the way soon, it'll get colonized? That every Haitian has a drum in his belly? Every Puerto Rican a fountain in his laughter? Every Cuban a sunbeam in his throat? Every Jamaican rum in his eyes? Every Dominican a heaven between his legs? Whoa, Chicha *loca*, I'm getting carried away . . . And stash *this* somewhere in your *guagua* noggin: those ideas are *received*, in fact they're spread by the media, especially the radio. And our chatterbox, among others, is currently raising a ruckus. Ah, you dimwit driver — received ideas? But Chicha, I admit that these jumbled ingredients — the belly-drum, fountain of laughter, sunny throat, rummy eyes, heavenly crotch — form the famous recipe for that eternal Fiesta of the Islands! And if we add the sulfur of Martinique,[19] the royal palm of Guadeloupe, and the other isles up and down the chain, we can serve up that incredible Caribbean Cocktail hot or cold, watered-down or a real eye-opener. Isn't that true, you dumb-derelict-Dominican-driver? Calm down, Chicha, I understand you, and very well, so well that I even wonder why we have to learn from a nor'wester that Trujillo knows the Mexican crooner Agustín Lara's "Song of Songs" by heart. Hey, Don Papito Consuelo Pipo y Gonzalez, my fine driver, that's enough to crack my pistons! Oh — I mean Solomon's, rather, excuse me, Chicha: sometimes I have holes in my head. All in all, Chicha, you're right. Because now that our people don't have a clue, here's the sarcastic-snitch-radio drumming into us that Don Pérez Agustín de Cortoba, all by himself, has lopped off five thousand different kinds of Haitian heads in Elías Piña: hot, bone, block, knuckle, air, pin, chowder, wooden, dunder, beetle, cabbage, sap, mutton, meat, muddle, bubble, pumpkin, feather, pig, mule, jug, blubber, pudding, bullet, flat, round, bald, square, pointy, fat, hang-dog, shame-faced, bewildered, empty, horse-faced, guilty, innocent, hatchet-faced, flighty, thick, dull, two-faced, high-brow, aching, pinch-faced, level, cool, lack-brained, slack-witted, numskulled, crackbrained, thimble-witted, addle-pated, pea-brained, feebleminded, beef-witted, rattle-brained, clod-pated, fuddle-brained, bird brains, dropped on their heads when they were young, with a price on them, keeping themselves down, keeping themselves above water, getting in over themselves, going off themselves, losing themselves, doomed to roll, and I don't know what-all!

The brazen, curt, grave tone drops a notch to announce:

"Confronted with the ambitions of the Third Reich, the League of Nations wonders and worries. Ten past five on our station with *Il Duce*."

The voice of the Italian strongman (it really is Mussolini, in fact) continues, more piping than brazen, curt, or grave: "Not a chance for freedom."

In any case, Don Pérez Agustín de Cortoba has cranked out five thousand different kinds of bodiless heads, dear Don Pipo, staunch Dominican that you are, so —

Heads up!

At the back of the *guagua* an adolescent is calmly working his way through a jar of guava jam. Way, way off in the distance, a quadrille is floating out into the hinterland, punctuated now and then by snatches of human voices.

"They dare to dance," muses Pedro Brito aloud.

"They are making death dance, monsieur," insists the man with the pipe. "That is the order: kill to the sound of music..."

"Jolly death!" wails Pedro Brito.

No one in the *guagua* wants to pursue this conversation, but all the passengers, even the children, have noticed the serious irritation of Chicha Calma, who has already slued around twice and is now churning everyone's bile with outrageous jolts. Gently, Chicha: *despacio,* my dear! Easy for you to say, my good *Dominicano,* but you're pretending not to hear the radio announcing at this very moment that Don Preguntas Feliz with his dirty fingernails has perforated ninety-seven little black girls from five to seven years old! I heard it, dear heart! In his delirium he mounted fifteen hundred Jamaican turkey-hens being fattened up for Christmas. I also heard that his horse had drunk up the wide river and the sky's reflection to boot. It's enough to jam all our pedals, Don Pipo — really, most excellent Pipo, enough to set our dials spinning! I can imagine, *señora,* that all this might pop the hood of the most sprightly of heavy vehicles, rattle the coolest of drivers, unsettle the sliest of smugglers, but what can we do? You're not going to have a tantrum, are you, my little bone-shaker, just because they're telling us that Haitian heads are marching silently through villages as a form of peaceful, unarmed protest? All that's none of my business, I agree, Doctor Pipo. Yes it is. Not a bit. Okay. No way — I'm just the border *guagua*. I come. I go. You plow up kilometers, Chicha *loca*, that's the least one can say! I exist in neutrality, Don Pipo, refusing to feed on political discourse, which says that our country has become both a vast torture chamber and an industrious bakery of poverty. That stinks of subversion, sweats contempt for authority, don't you think? Don't worry, you yellow-belly — Chicha, I'm here to bear witness that you simply load up in Hinche, unload in Ouanaminthe, wait around in Boc Banic, toss one back in Honda Valle, picnic in Fond-des-Chênes, bathe in Yabanico, sleep in Pedernales. You can say that again! I, Chicha Calma, I know them, those little places tucked away along the border, and that mixed bag of people all tangled together. Jimaní smells like cassava and rushes. The girls in Belladère have breasts like — hey, Monsieur Pipo, you dirty old man, you're speeding, driving me too hard and wearing me out. You want to get us killed?

"Actually, am I not soliloquizing again? Is it the effect of what could be called driver's loneliness? You can get a touch of loneliness just as you get a touch of sunstroke. And that multiplies your head," murmurs Pipo. He clears his throat: "For now, I'm staying away from daydreams."

As proud as a girl from Santiago, the *guagua* barrels along, zooming through the pre-dawn air. Elías Piña isn't far. But there's no hovering scent of chamomile, no tantalizing aroma of cornbread, and where's the familiar hum like the buzzing of countless wings pillaging vast flourishing gardens? A dense silence engulfs the *guagua*. Everyone is afraid to think about this . . . Everyone is ashamed. As if the most loathsome murder were within oneself.

Meanwhile, dawn is blushing. A flock of crows is pecking apart the sky. Shards of azure flecked with blood rain down. The middle-aged man puffs faster and faster on his pipe. *Nervioso*. The little *india* girl asks to go peepee. No one listens to her. The driver's mustachioed head floors the accelerator. It takes your breath away! His Dominican driver's head is just eating up the kilometers. Kilometers of horizons. Canefields. Open country out on a spree.

The rooster tied somewhere up on the luggage rack launches his cock-a-doodle-doo, and dies.

Carried off by the dawn.

Elías Piña, the Dominican border town with the white wooden chapel, dusty streets, rusty roofs, the smell of chamomile and cornbread, the rickety little iron bridge, and the fountain with a pink sandstone basin, enters the treads of Chicha Calma's tires.

Pedro Brito turns pale.

Mussolini's voice hammers the passengers' heads: "Towards eternal strength, brutal and heroic." Don Pipo turns off the engine. Chicha shudders for a moment, then subsides. The only radio in Elías Piña takes over. Il Duce is in full cry.

Dominican journalists claim that Trujillo models himself

on the lord of Italy. The only things missing are the helmet plume and the bantam strut. He's already got the boots, they point out.

Don Pérez Agustín de Cortoba, cartridges at his belt, machete in hand, his right eye bloodshot, stands in the middle of Elías Piña's main street continuing his voyage between Emmanuela's legs. This time, however, he notices that the long, slender legs are not really answering his call, neither gripping nor purging his immense beige body. Something tells him that Emmanuela has passed on in the massacre, even though she left Dominican territory long before it broke out. When he met her three months ago, somewhere between the two countries, he never imagined she would wind up this way. Everything about her was pleasure, song, hot-blooded excitement! Now he must seek his satisfaction all by himself, since even his phantasms have dropped him.

Don Agustín snarls and flees. Take that! cries the machete.

—20—

No matter how hard Adèle tries to get hold of her head, put it back on, shove it down on her shoulders, nail it, cement it, rivet it to her neck, the head still capers about, bounding over the fence of candelabra cacti into the dust-white street, the main street of Elías Piña, where Don Pérez Agustín de Cortoba's house is fidgeting in its bath of whitewash. Feeling whimsical, Adèle's head sticks out its tongue at some children, who've gone back to throwing dust in one another's eyes.

One of them, a little brown guy, thinks he's a cabbage. He spends a good minute forming a head. When he feels he's round enough, he leafs out. To do this, he delivers a flurry of bites to his shoulders, arms, or hands about every five minutes, so that an hour later, he's covered in blood. Amused, his friends dance around him clapping and singing:

Red cabbage, white cabbage,
Savoy cabbage, Chinese cabbage,
Rutabaga!
You're good for soup.

Seized with religious fervor, Adèle's head darts into the church, teases a devil on the holy-water basin, and sets the bells to ringing their heads off.

Pedro gives a start. Just like two years ago, when we joined our lives in the tiny pink-brick chapel in Maïssade, you in white organdy, on the arm of your father, Señor Aristide Benjamin, a farmer in Belladère, I in a snuff-colored suit, on the arm of my mother, Señora Mercedes Altagracia Brito y Molina, a secondhand dealer in Jimaní. Laughter was the order of the day. In the small chapel, flowers hung from a blue sky sprinkled with white stars: armfuls of tuberoses, bunches of lilacs, bouquets of wild roses. Plucked by some mysterious flutter of wings, petals floated just above our heads in a kind of shifting and perfumed ceiling. The aging mahogany harmonium gargled out an ancient Andalusian love song. The saints, angels, and cherubs sneaked glances at one another, clearly happy to see so many people gathered together to solemnize this union. Blonde Lucy in particular, in her voluminous blue cloak, flashed her smile at Andrew, bleeding like a poppy in his maroon coat. And when *el padre* César López y Contrario asked us to exchange vows, I thought I glimpsed in your eyes a flicker of hesitation. The chapel was suddenly empty, deserted. God's altar had collapsed. But when amid the thicket of candles you smiled at me in acceptance, God's wine went to my head. Without being asked I drank water from your mouth. Now time has rolled up its mat and withdrawn, leaving us the debris of its passage and our aching hearts. Are we a mirage on the surface of its reality?

Leaving the holy place where the bells are still pealing, the head, going its own libertine way, begins to dance a merengue — writhing and wriggling, twisting and twirling, stretching, shrinking — and shamelessly latches on to an *indio* lieutenant, who bites its tongue back to the uvula.

You have never been so sensual, even on that honeymoon evening when you bled my neck with dainty nips. From your oh-so-small and delicate teeth, and I still don't know where you ever got those beauties. Your milk-teeth, nibbling so pleasantly . . .

Pedro prepares to leave the *guagua* but, stayed by a friendly hand, sits down again automatically, obeying the gesture of the middle-aged man, who puffs harder and harder on his pipe. "To think that they pulled it off, *los diablos!*" groans the man hoarsely.

Adèle tries grabbing her head, screwing it onto her neck, soldering it, putting on her cayman-skin sandals to captivate and tame it, singing a sentimental song about orange blossoms to recover it — but in vain: the head goes head-over-heels, teeters, capsizes, enters an establishment purveying strong drink, downs a neat shot, coughs. *¡Fuerte, mi hombre!* Like the flamed brandy you drank every evening after work. *¡Bien fuerte, mi hombre!* And, darting under the skirt of an old negress, the head giggles: "Peek-a-boo!"

Even there you can't behave, you cheeky *morena!*

When Pedro tries again to rise, an inexplicable force holds him back as his legs buckle beneath him.

The middle-aged man can't manage to move either, of course. His mind's in a muddle. His pipe has gone out, but it's still clamped firmly in the corner of his mouth.

The driver is frozen in place, with the taste of vinegar in the back of his throat.

Not a soul moves in the *guagua.*

Still seated, they stare transfixed at Adèle's antics. One passenger has a humming in his ears, another's mouth is dry. This one is dizzy, that one has a migraine. They feel nauseated. They're shaking. They've got stomach cramps. They're sweating bullets. They're terrified.

Mussolini retires. Replaced by a baseball game. You can hear stadium noise in the background. In Chicago, it seems. "The Yankees take on the Cubs," brays the announcer.

Bang in the middle of the dusty main street of Elías Piña, Chicha Calma looks like a pop sculpture featuring the stiff, slim legs of the *negrita* sticking out a window in a V next to the rooster, which hangs by its feet in cadaverous rigidity, wings outspread like a fan, plus, in rows of five on ten benches, the petrified passengers. Ever since I can remember, which means since 1918, I, Chicha Calma, who have never run out of gas, Ford *guagua* No. 2742 (113 tickets, 16 top-to-bottom-tune-ups, 15 dead batteries, 6 on-board radios kaput, 8 motor conk-outs, 432 flat tires), I never could stand standing still. I am a progressive *guagua.* I rebel against all sorcery that would keep me in one place. Do I look like I'm ready for a strait jacket? A zombi? Me? Come off it! Not on your life! But who or what is holding our people in thrall? Weird, isn't it? Maybe a mass fit? What old folks call a seizure?

"Everyone's catatonic, Chicha!" thinks the driver. "Whoops — I'm skidding again . . . Really, I keep on talking for Chicha and me both," he rethinks, as if deeply at fault.

Adèle's head meets another head. What a mug on that one! Why's it flapping its ears around? Must be some kind of donkey complex! "Sunilda? Nuri? What's gotten into *la cabeza de* Doña Clairmise? I mean, talk about funny!"

Adèle's nosy head takes off, nostrils flared, all eyes, ears to the wind. Leaping from arcade to arcade, it reaches the courthouse, a crumbling edifice of gray concrete, and starts right in demanding justice for Doña Clairmise's jug-handle ears, as well as for the round and ruddy noodle of Father Ramírez, freshly arrived in a cloud of dust. Me, Adèle's head, a Christian, a citizen, in the name of conscience, I protest! Adèle's head gets a resounding slap. In the name of national dignity. Adèle's head lowers its eyes. Of human rights. And slinks away, crestfallen. Of democracy. What did the good Father Ramírez, so thin in his cassock, ever do to them? Lousy scum! Adèle's head hobbles off to hide like a sulking kitty atop the covered porch of an old pinewood house that has been three-quarters destroyed by fire. Of the emancipation of the sexes. Two years spent by your side without even a hint of a nasty look, a threat, or a blow, my man! My man shipwrecked by dawn. Those bastards!

Frightened, Adèle huddles lower and lower on the porch. Never has she felt so alone, so abandoned. Those dirty gangsters! I cannot find last night's perfume, the streets have shrouded themselves, you carried everything away with you into the dawn.

The head leaves the dilapidated house, which has

collapsed enough to reveal, in a Louis XVI parlor, a little old couple, killed during their siesta. Taken by surprise, without enough time to hold hands and say goodbye.

¡Diablo! Limping, Adèle's head toddles off toward the candy-pink public fountain set in the middle of a small public square of beaten earth, showered with sunshine.

"*¡Dios!* What are you doing here, *cabecita de* Pablocito? Your little head is Dominican! Hey! You're kidding me! Unbelievable! Pablocito, you mean that a native like you couldn't frigging manage to say *perejil* correctly? A *pequeño blanco de la tierra como tù?... ¡Entonces, Pablocito!*"

Adèle's head glug-glugs its fill. So do Zaba, *el hijo de* Doña Isabela; *José, el sobrino de* Don Amílcar; Roberto, *el primo de* Papito Gómez. Native son, nephew, cousin: incapable of saying *perejil*. In that case, there's good reason to fear for Pedro. Lost in the dawn. His scent had lingered in the bedroom a long time after his departure, the smell of a hardworking man. Gone off to meet with others, to talk. His story had filled the bedroom, so that I heard the workers' voices. That morning, Pedro had the face of those tall, gentle people who are only sixteen but seem thirty years old. Dawn tagged along behind him; his footsteps crossed the horizon. My mutilated love! So who will have heard the last cry? Seen that last look in the night? Neighbor, don't you think it's all this that has unhinged me, more than I was before? Dawn has some strange tricks up its sleeve, I'm telling you, Pedro!

Stooped, bent nearly double, the head dashes here, runs there. Déclassé. Trots, light-headed. Skips about, scatty.

Jumps in astonishment, olé! Goes off on an inspection tour, posthaste. *Vaya,* little inspector head! It berates a blundering mouth. Sets straight a disoriented pair of saffron-yellow legs. Tickles the cute cheeks of a *niño*. Imitates a machete. Hey, hop! Hey, hop! Turns the back of its neck on a *guardia*. Wipes a face clean of pus. Quickens its pace. Approaches the *guagua,* and stops. But hesitates. Purrs. Timidly.

"Don't be scared, you can come inside, Señora Adèle. Don't be afraid of Chicha, or of me, her driver. We're in the same fix: we're all topsy-turvy. (Pause.) You, just possibly, a bit more than most . . ."

"We all go off the rails sometimes, conductor, otherwise how could you explain the fact that we sleep with the gods and invite the sky to our table?"

"That's right, *señora!* We live in a land of legends. Therefore our speech goes backward. We live in the bird and the flower, in travel and wine."

"A *people* are never crazy, jalopy-driver! Neurotic is another story. Adolf Hitler's Germans show a tendency to hysteria. The American North is full of suckers, while the South has hotheads. But they're not nuts for a second. Neither are we, even though we do believe that trees can think. People say that every evening, the giant *mapou*[20] at the Biliguy crossroads takes a walk in its astral body: a round light, thirty centimeters in diameter, dull blue (representing femininity, it seems), with orange flecks in the center. A flitting, glimmering light. Like me, Adèle, the Rival of dawn."

"The things folks say! We are a people of enchanters, we

bring everything to life: jugs, drums, flags, music, perfumes, wooden statues, forests, sunbeams, rivers, colors, even the stuffed crows guarding Vodou temples."

"Not forgetting old rattletraps, right, junkheap? We make them talk, comment, analyze, act. Didn't Amédée Beauzile de Thiotte recently give a good-luck bath[21]

(10 pinches of flour from France
20 ounces of Florida water
4 handfuls of orange blossoms
2 coffee spoons of ammonia
7 white roses
6 red roses
3 yellow roses
2 thunderstones
8 pints of white rum
the heads of 15 mud hens
as much *roroli* as the *houngan* feels is necessary
all mixed up in a big bathtub full of Dutch beer)

to his *guagua,* Las Flores, so she would run better and attract more clients? It's no secret, the whole border knows about it. They even say the wind took part in the ceremony as a medium."

"— As a chatterbox, scandalmonger, *hablador!* Chicha, my *guagua,* knows the wind better than anybody. It's a blabber, the wind! A tattletale! A windbag! A humbug *rabòdiò!* And when it gets together with the radio — watch out . . ."

"That's it, driver — a gossip! We bring the wind to life as well, the wind and the seas. We're a fanciful people! Women and the morning dew!"

"Hallucination or not (I know that the *señora* is loony or manic-depressive, I'll leave it at that), I, Don Pipo, driver of a border *guagua*, I can vouch for Señor Pedro's love. The plains, mornes, savannas, valleys I have crossed will bear witness to that man's affection for you. He carries you the way a watch carries the time. Mindlessly. Without considering happiness or disaster. Madly. Now that we're being forced (Chicha and I) to cast off our lines, we're left adrift, mere observers of a vast upheaval. One is not always master of one's fate, you see! And every case is different. *¡Bueno!* You'll notice that I'm foregoing all lyricism. Simply keeping track. In my sorry state. But I will say that in the whole time I have known Chicha (speed 160 kilometers per hour, over 1.4 million kilometers on the odometer), she has never been so brutally shoved aside. Really, without any respect or consideration for her quarter-century of service! From Mancenille to Pedernales. From the throaty laughter of the Atlantic to the hubbub of the Caribbean Sea! (More or less!)"

Adèle's head looks all around for a long time. As if in a dream.

Don Pipo's *guagua* enriches its pop-sculpture allure: hissing, the right rear tire goes flat. A swirling smell of roses explodes, streaking the air with shards. The head shakes itself. Why this noise inside me as if I were possessed by a thousand haunted things? The old house completes its fall into ruin; the couple, in their suspended animation, keep seeking the warmth of their sundered bond. I wander from one street to another, searching for some sign of the right address. Pedro tries to stand up. My shipwreck is scouring ever greater depths. To run toward Adèle. Wherever have you banked your fire? Cannot manage it. To make me shiver so. Glued to his seat. When everything is festively ablaze with noon. The head plunges into the *guagua*. You're going to break your paws, my love, schizophrenic little beast! Alights on the right shoulder of the middle-aged man, whose pipe is going out, tucked into the corner of his mouth. "So they've sunk to that, the bullies!" The head goes over to feel the body of the young woman . . . And jumps back. Asks to speak again to the driver now asleep at the wheel. Or dead. No one can say exactly what has suddenly happened to the driver.

The head, unbalanced, drones beneath the ceiling of the *guagua*. It's a fly, a honey-beam, or a small soul in torment.

(My younger sister, Léone, with hair like a raven's wing, who died last March, before her birthday, is circling the electric lamp. She reminds me of those fires in the night, snuffed out, that leave no memory behind.)

The head snuggles up to Pedro Brito. I've been thinking about the song we love. Rocks to and fro. The wounds have grown wider, as if everything coming from you had the taste of slaughter. Quivers. It's no use my preparing the altar for us to lie upon as one flesh. Slumps. But the memory of our passion simply refuses to be sacrificed. The head recoils. Pedro Brito would like to touch it, take it, hold it, honor it. Such a flower must cross itself when the crucified remains pass between us. The head grows mournful. My love! The seed we thought would grow is rotting. The head sags. The earth holds its funereal note, and I feel the fear of being torn asunder stirring in you. Pedro opens his arms to caress Adèle. *¡Un doloroso cariño!* Pedro Alvarez Brito y Molina's arms remain outstretched, like a crossbeam. Your tears, and mine, in vain. Leaving the *guagua,* the head returns to the streets.

O etherized Adèle, consigned to unremitting madness!

Nailed to his seat, Pedro Brito watches Adèle's head busily accompany others — this one to the police station, that one to the presbytery, another one to the schoolhouse, yet another to the clinic, and another to the white wooden chapel. *Vaya bien,* little community-activist head! *Vaya, negrita mía.*

Meanwhile, Wrigley Stadium is in a ferment. The sound of firecrackers mingles with the pealing of Elías Piña's church bells. Which makes a helluva racket.

Having buzzed its fill around hundreds of heads — Pierre Delatour, the tailor in Las Matas; Dieudonné Darbouze, the blacksmith in Limón; Sylvio Joseph, the farmer in Baní — and hobnobbed aplenty with heads from Maribaroux, Commendadore, Vallière, Ferrier, and Capotille, Adèle's head leans against the candy-pink house of Preguntas Feliz and dozes, dead beat.

It dreams of the orange shirt of coarse linen that had possessed her, really and truly! Then, her eyes had rolled back to see a time of rainy weather, her nostrils had breathed in every garden perfume, her tongue had tripped the light fantastic, her body had thrilled to a strange tingling.

Adèle sees her belly swell like a melon and Pedro measuring off on her rounded body the eight ells of sky-blue calico he'd bought in the market at Fond-Parisien.

That lasts a good minute, during which the street, finally freed from Adèle's antics, interrupts the baseball game for a bulletin *del Departamento del interior y de la Defensa Nacional:*

"We are in a position to announce to the Dominican nation at large, and to the border people in particular, that Operation *Cabezas Haitianas* has gone precisely as planned, without a hitch, despite the senseless and systematic socialist opposition of certain Dominican workers led by Guillermo Sánchez y Santana and Pedro Alvarez Brito y Molina."

Adèle winds herself up in the wave of blue cloth, while into her outspread arms fall green birds tumbling from the sky with billowing clouds and seas.

The one-and-only radio chants:

"We were able to identify those double-troublemakers in time, and our machetes have trimmed about sixty thousand necks."

Some heads that have been wandering the streets of Elías Piña for a while stop in their tracks. Flabbergasted.

The applause in Wrigley Field picks up again. The Yankees appear to have scored a run. Adèle drapes the sea around her shoulders and while she's at it, adds Don Agustín de Cortoba's epaulets. The noise from the stadium in Chicago dies down. The radio reports:

"We are pleased, in addition, to inform the Dominican people that Port-au-Prince is not planning any retaliation, aside from a slight show of saber-rattling put on by a small group of soldiers, peasants, and poets. And that in any case, as we have already mentioned, the Dominican army is on the border, prepared for any eventuality."

Adèle tears the blue material, scattering the birds and flames to the four winds, which had come running to enjoy the bloodshed.

"The Haitian administration, from the Foreign Minister to the Typing Pool, including Cabinet Officers, Bureau Chiefs, and Permanent Under-Secretaries, attended a reception in the National Palace, Champs de Mars, Place des Héros, on the very day Operation *Cabezas Haitianas* began."

The heads topple over into the dust.

"That morning, a *Te Deum* was celebrated in the Basilica of Notre-Dame in Port-au-Prince in honor, it seems, of the ninety-seventh birthday of the chief of state's sister. On that occasion, nineteen battalions of khaki-clad infantry with fixed bayonets, preceded by fifteen mounted officers, paraded through the streets of the capital to the applause of children who expected these armed men to change at any minute into toy soldiers."

Adèle covers herself from head to toe. Through the blue cloth, she sees the sword-blades foaming.

"Incidentally, the Dominican people might be interested to know that as each Haitian head fell here, a glass of champagne over there turned red . . ."

Two days ago, on the very eve of the massacre, a masked ball for civil servants was given in the president's palace. More national heroes attended than foxes, spiders, skunks, jackals, hyenas, monkeys, or wolves, for the sole and simple reason that some Haitians have always considered themselves better than others.

And a perfect fit for the role of gallant champions!

Toussaint Louverture, in full fig as Governor-General-for-Life (boots, frock coat, bicorne, stars and oak-leaf clusters) sipped a gin à l'orange that turned strangely sticky. Plain old blood!

A cawing crow strolled by, bleeding a flood of Barbancourt rum from his beak.

When the bugle hanging on the sickly green wall of the guard room saw Jean-Jacques Dessalines gulp plasma from a glass of cognac, it trumpeted its lungs out, while the electric lights in the halls shriveled in their sockets.

Poisoned, some rat or other (or perhaps a cockroach — there was a bit of everything there that night) stained his whiskers with a cochineal-red liquid. No doubt about it: a Bloody Martini!

A calf with the staggers chewed clots swimming in cherry brandy.

Reptiles left scarlet trails reeking of Pernod.

Costumed as a cockatoo, a Symbolist poet of the '30s showed off his mercurochrome jabot and informed anyone who would listen that his wife (a nanny goat) was jealous of his concubine (a bitch-dog) and had just hurled a liter of Johnny Walker Blood-Red Label at his head.

With one accord, the merrymakers poured the drinks into an enormous brass cauldron, splashing themselves so thoroughly that they were sopping wet in no time, and in their trance crushed myriads of globules between their fingers.

The Symbolist poet swore on the head of the President of the Republic that the performance was worthy of the Age of Dionysus.

In the ballroom, the red glow grew ever fiercer as Haitian heads rolled in Mamaya, La Loma, Lacrou, Santo Pedro, those villages living along the border.

Alexandre Pétion [22] knocked back so much Dom Perignon he thought he was a butcher, and called for cutlass, saw, and cleaver, while a rumpled-looking grouse covered him with sticking plasters to stem the blood welling from his every pore.

As a Haitian head went flying in Las Matas, the white wine in the glass of His Majesty Henri I of Haiti effervesced with bright red bubbles!

For each Haitian decapitation at the border, a draught of Haitian blood at the masked ball, Field of Mars, Square of Heroes.

That same night, a military dance was held in another room of the presidential palace. No masks there — only uniforms, salutes, serenity, and decorum. Alcoholic beverages were forbidden, of course, but through priggish precaution, all liquids of any kind were banished: fizzy drinks, fruit juices, water, mineral water, coconut milk, milk (whole, skim, condensed, evaporated, pasteurized, and chocolate), coffee, café au lait, cocoa, vegetable juices, the whole shooting match.

On the other hand, there was a lavish spread of pastas and

baked goods: fritters, noodles, tarts, vermicelli, macaroni, spaghetti, cakes, pastries, dainties galore!

Music by turns rousing and sentimental sent couples twirling and promenading around the floor, as the teasing of taffeta flirted with the clinking of swords. The trilling of feminine voices softened the rigidity of discipline. Gourmets plied their knives and forks with a will.

The army was enjoying itself.

A few guests were worried, however: the pastries were behaving rather strangely. A sergeant-major eating a piece of sweetsop pie snapped his right upper canine on a flat bone, probably a patella. A captain eating a slice of cake exclaimed at the juiciness of a morsel of roast veal, earning an indulgent smile from an elderly retired colonel relishing some particularly tender hamburger in his pudding.

A corporal sucked on a caramel that tasted deliciously of breaded piglet's testicle; in San Francisco de Macorís, a Dominican *guardia* astride the thighs of a Haitian cane-cutter was slicing off his balls.

The fact is that every time a Haitian was hacked apart at the border, flesh turned up in a pastry at the military ball: roasted (at the correct temperature), fried (with very little fat), braised (for tougher items requiring slow cooking), poached (the ever-popular pot-au-feu).

The soldiers adapted to this metamorphosis in progress, and wishing to turn it to full advantage, they appealed to an expert, who explained the ritual of carving.

So listen to the expert carver:

"A meal, no matter how private, is an occasion for gathering together, and the skillful carving of a roast enhances these moments of communion. For centuries, in fact, the art of carving with subtlety and refinement was considered an indispensable accomplishment in a man."

The speaker was interrupted by a young lieutenant in a snug and spotless uniform.

"Get to the point!" he exclaimed, his eyes like glittering slits.

Listen as the expert raised his voice:

"For greatest efficiency, employ a large fork, to hold the meat, and a very sharp knife."

"We're beginning to get the idea, forge ahead!" laughed a gap-toothed captain.

Listen as the chef forged ahead:

"In addition to good utensils, one must possess a precise knowledge of the conformation of the meat. When you carve, avoid piercing the meat too deeply with the fork: the teeth will tear holes and waste some of the juices."

A major's wife, immense in a pastel-blue spangled dress, threw a gastronomic fit:

"Stop! Water! Water! My mouth is watering! Stop it — get some fire, to stop my mouth from watering!"

She was led from the room.

Listen to the carver soldier on:

"If the roast is grilled or quite rare, your slices may be relatively thick, for it is harder to slice pink or red meat, since the texture is less firm. On the other hand, you may easily cut cold roast beef, even when rare, into very thin slices."

The master carver saluted, salivated, and sighed, "I have spoken. Dinner is served."

And looked all around him, beaming.

The room exploded in bravos, bubbling with delight as the guests applauded and fussed over the Master. Wily and sanctimonious, he confessed that the description of the ritual was not his, but the work of the famous author of *On Beef and Veal*. The applause grew louder. The chef was showered with compliments as the guests sliced eagerly into the organ meats: liver, heart, kidneys, tripe, and other offal.

While Dominican machetes were hacking away at Haitian muscles over there, in the villages along the border.

The servants in the two ballrooms called the festivities shameful treason: "You've enjoyed the fruits of our nation's harvests without turning over one clod of our soil. What are we in your eyes? Fodder for forced labor? You hear our suffering with contempt. You compare our country to others and spit upon her, but we must truly love it, for we have never abandoned her. We revel in our limpid skies, our heads swim with the sweet smells of our mountains. So when we see you tearing the country to pieces, we curse you! How can we get rid of you?"

Regarding the metamorphosis of the refreshments, the radio station *La Voz Dominicana* announces coldly:

"According to observers, it was a clear sign that Haiti's tutelary gods were angry."

The heads dig their hole. The piece of blue calico sags.

Adèle buries herself in it, more and more lost in the dream she's dreaming of.

La Voz Dominicana piles it on:

"The highly sensitive citizens of the Dominican Republic have no doubt quickly grasped what we need not point out: the Haitian authorities abandoned the Haitian border people."

The heads pile up in their hole. Bow their heads in shame, sorrowing for themselves. Adèle has broken the wing of a green bird.

"We wash our hands of this," concludes *La Voz Dominicana,* adding, "Coca-Cola, hits the spot! Weather: same as before."

The whole thing bears the signature of the Great Torturer. Who has worked his torturous will. To his own satisfaction.

The bells jabber away even more merrily. One of them seems to be hovering over the *guagua,* twittering, leaping, and larking about until it flies into a thousand fulminating fragments, rocketing into a steel-blue sky whose one fixed point is the bird-emblem, while stray dogs fight in vain over the raptor's shadow. A distant voice is almost lost in this din.

"The next of kin will be notified in cases of decerebration."

Adèle's head bursts from its dream, opening its eyes.

The street-radio adds, as an afterthought:

"Or evisceration."

Then crackles with discordant cries. Then closes with the Yankees and the Cubs in Wrigley Field. Then goes off the air.

There's no need for any more bulletins from the authorities. The whole affair is a done deal. The people have been told enough. The League of Nations will make a fuss, that's understandable, but after a few diplomatic formalities that haven't changed since Cyrus the Great, it will all be forgotten.

Case closed.

The press and airwaves will now observe an appropriate silence.

That epidemic of silence once envisaged by a young officer stationed in Azua . . .

Then Adèle's head peremptorily reclaims its rights: it's off, zipping here-there-and-everywhere, panting, laughing, taking stock. I'll do better than this when I've had my kid, even though my womb has never wanted to grow my man's seed. The head twirls around, flashing a set of sparkling teeth. As in Maribaroux, when you danced among the parrots in your white dress of broderie anglaise. Hops. Your slim ebony legs blazed beneath your skirt. Pirouettes. Your footsteps had the electric energy of a beehive. The bees have moved up into my attic. My family and I cannot contain such heaps of luck, music, golden sky. Giddiness is difficult to bear when it comes from on high. We feel as if we have chanced upon happiness. I breathe deeply, and live on the delight of my eyes. My child will be called Rafael.

Reaching out through the only window in the whitewashed house of Don Pérez Agustín de Cortoba, the bare arm of a light-skinned woman empties a basin of dirty water into the courtyard of large yellow bricks. A couple of jackdaws caw. The same cold, detached voice blurts out:

"A few pesos will take care of everything."

No! Not like the Torturer, what was I thinking of! Rafael Trujillo! *¡Coñaso!* Oh, *perdóname, mi viejo*. Forgive me, husband, you know I've never used vulgar words — me, Adèle Benjamin, before God and the Republic — or behaved shamelessly. *Yo lo juro. ¡Sí, lo juro!* I swear on the head of my father, *el señor* Aristide Benjamin, farmer in Belladère. *¡Muy santa soy yo!* But the fate I've been handed, Papito! . . . The head rears back, showing a strong, smooth throat. My boy will bear the name of Guillermo, *el jefe!* The man who gave the cane a human face. Guillermo! The man who spoke to the cane, so that it could understand, and set itself on fire. The blazing stalks sputter, sway in terror, clatter threateningly, then trample the night in closed ranks. The theoretician complains of anarchy, not knowing that day breaks in sacrifice to the dawn. The head turns swiftly, revealing a strand of rosy shells around its neck. You've never been funnier. You remember thumbing your nose at that country policeman? Whirls around. Your breasts were bouncing with glee. I've always kept your supper, *la comida tuya,* warm for you. Your lips were trembling with delight. I've always starched things properly. Your eyes were blazing. Ironed your overalls. Capers. The laundry area smelled of vetiver, and the particular mustiness of a well. Staggers, hiding a gentle tear. You would shake the water drops from the well-worn clothing. They splattered in rainbow-glinting stars on your bare feet.

Playfully, the head wags its tongue. You're still turning my head with your crazy-little-girl ways. Grins, exults, rejoices. And you, you lumbering great factory worker, how you got me going in Maribaroux with your huge paw on my hips! The age spots on the face of President Franklin Delano Roosevelt, splashed in color across dozens of magazine covers, outshone the red-faced tomatoes that had come to market from so far away . . . from Marmelade (you remember?), high among the clouds. Among the springs. A scrawny, deaf yellow dog dragged his miserable solitude around. You, singing, teasing, shouting, joking, you sank your teeth into a steaming, half-cooked haunch of goat. You vampire, you!

Seven close-shaven black heads pass by, zigzagging, as if lost, bumping into one another, each clenching between its teeth a twenty-peso bill: *Banco Central de la República Dominicana Veinte Pesos de Oro*. The price agreed upon by the Haitian government for a Haitian neck, for Haitian organs, for a Haitian memory. A Haitian ass. Port-au-Prince didn't bother with ways or means or routine protocol. Or even bluffing, grandstanding, putting up a front. Port-au-Prince didn't go in for hypocrisy, swaggering, righteous wrath, curses, sanctimony, gloating: it was all the same to them, business as usual. An invoice, a bill.

"The Dominican government undertakes to pay an indemnity of $750,000 which the Haitian government is free to employ in the best interests of those persons who have experienced injury or loss during these events."

Voilà! The League of Nations is satisfied. That's the way it has been ever since the Queen of Sheba.

Like taking a piss.

Like clockwork.

As if pigs could fly. As if wishes were horses. Feelings, positive or negative — esteem, contempt, indignation, admiration: zilch!

That tens of thousands of skulls are knocking about, rattling around, clonking into one another — *basta!* So what! Port-au-Prince has cashed in, no muss, no fuss, no delegation, no ceremony, no special delivery. No formal receipt. No sealed envelope. Just handed over directly. A grocer's change: twenty pesos for a head. Port-au-Prince is preening itself. And Port-au-Prince may well preen itself. It won't be long before we see some high-ranking army officer build a brand-new villa on the Colline de la Coupe; the windows of a new store owned by a Communal Councilor glinting on the Place Notre-Dame de l'Assomption; the official mistress of the Secretary of State taking a steamer to Europe; a senator of the Republic gliding through the streets of the capital in his factory-fresh limousine; a flurry of bank accounts opening in Switzerland.

Considering what the bill for those people came to, they could hardly expect us to leave them a tip.

—21—

In desperation, and to console himself for his disappointment, Rafael Leónidas Trujillo y Molina set himself to considering the jasper, copperas, porphyry, alabaster, gold, rock crystal, silver, rubies, diamonds, jet, opals, asbestos, and the magnetic ore of Cotuí that brighten the subsoil of his country. To thinking about the mighty horses of the Cibao Valley, the donkeys of Azua and Baní, the pigs and goats of Neiba, the sparrows, peacocks, woodpeckers, and falcons that throng the forests; the agoutis, iguanas, *morrocoi* tortoises, and red land crabs that thrive in the groves of palm trees; the trout, red mullet, and swordfish of the seas around Monte Cristi and San Pedro de Macorís. To reviewing the mahogany of the forests of Azua, Bahoruco, Puerto Plata, and La Yuna, and such woods as *espinille, capá,* cedar, carob, pine, *catey* (which when polished resembles tortoiseshell), ebony, *cavina, tabaco* (prized for fine furniture), and *nazareno,* with its violet burl. To tallying up the trees — medlar, orange, rose apple, lemon, sapodilla plum — that flourish in season on Dominican soil. To inventorying exports: tobacco, honey, starch, cotton, coffee, and divi-divi pods used in tanning; horned animals and the hides of cattle, goats, sheep; copper, liquor, coconut oil, raw sugar, molasses, tortoiseshell, Jamaica wood, and lignum vitae.

Standing surrounded by Dominican national heroes, the Generalissimo reviewed his troops: in Azua, the Ligero, Regulares, and Chavalos battalions; in Santiago, the light infantry battalions of the Yaque; in Puerto Plata, the battalion of San Felipe; in Higüey, the Salvaleón; in Los Llanos, the bloodthirsty Sangriento; and finally, battalions of light infantry in La Vega, Monte Cristi, Neiba, and Samaná.

He had devoted long hours to studying the customs of his country. Had discovered that he was the leader of a people who were hospitable, unselfish, effusive, quarrelsome, fond of games of chance, horse races, cockfights. People who made love with real heart — and bared fangs.

To possess his entire land, he had galloped the length and breadth of it. Like a conquistador. Vast plains with lofty mountains. The trade winds had told him the stories of Caonabo, of Nuñez de Cáceres,[23] and spoken of the four great rivers and three thousand lesser ones flecked with gold dust. On Monte Tina (3,190 meters), he had contemplated his nation with its horizons of land, sky, and sea. He could embrace all these marvels at his leisure . . .

Despite his monopoly on metals, minerals, salt marshes, birds, reptiles, fish, insects, vegetables; his stranglehold on agriculture, industry, commerce, finance, the armed forces; his grip on Dominican mores, arts, letters, religion, public education, justice; his influence on the population and dominance of the country; his titles, medals, mistresses, and bodyguards . . . despite all this, Rafael Leónidas Trujillo y Molina suffered from Citadel sickness. He could not bring himself to accept that the fortress did not belong to him. Eventually, he began to bear a terrific grudge against the Haitian people.

He had received his order of weapons, of course. He had received arms of all kinds, of all horrors. But he had no real need to wage war to obtain Haitian flesh. The authorities in Port-au-Prince supplied him with some at every sugar-cane harvest.

On those occasions, thousands of government agents scoured the towns and countryside, trumpeting that *la zafra,* the cane-cutting, was about to begin in the Dominican Republic. That workers could grow rich simply by harvesting cane, because such work paid much more than peasant farming. And that over there, white women were as thick on the ground as grass.

That said, Haitians agreed to go next-door. In the meantime, they were photographed: 6 gourdes for a half-dozen shots, full-face. They received their identity cards: 3.50 gourdes at the inaccessible windows of the Tax Office, 15 to 20 gourdes on the black market. Their fingerprints were placed on a yellow index card along with the acquired, imagined, created data of their criminal records (misdemeanors, crimes, fines, sentences, acquittals — the works) and civil status: marriage, concubinage, number of children, the whole ball and chain.

After nights of waiting on the pavement at the hiring locations, the workers would be packed into trucks and dumped out in Dominican territory. Rubbing their hands in glee, the middlemen calculated their commissions, percentages, bonuses, tips, bribes. That's it for another season!

See you next time, *compadre!*

To tell the truth, Haitian laborers weren't worried about going to the Dominican Republic, because at home, poverty was served up hot or cold every hour of the day and night. So Trujillo's men treated the Haitian peasants with both the disdain of the privileged and the arrogance of *blancos de la tierra*.

Over the years, the Dominican authorities would have ample supplies of submissive proletarian flesh, docile wielders of hungry machetes. Every morning, before the raising of the flag, Dominican schoolchildren would hear harangues about the Haitian devil, *el diablo haitiano*. They would learn to hate Haitian children, despise Haitian women, mock the Haitian elderly, curse Haitian men. The authorities would make those themes the backbone of their political party. One of Trujillo's many improvisations would be: "Remember that the island awakens in the East and that the land of our neighbors is the haunt of shadows."

That attitude would inspire the schemes of the Dominican authorities.

An attitude of *carte blanche*.

—22—

Freed from the spell that had bound him to his seat, Pedro Brito stands up. Walks. Toward the shooting-star head of Adèle. Which stops careening around. Ponders. *Mi hijo* — Pedrocito's what his name will be! Like you, *otro jefe, como tú!* My son will take up the slack in the rope, he'll take up the story again, he'll take up the burden and because he will make the sun rise, *el hijo mío* will take up the journey again with clear vision, with what's needed, with the consent and determination of the others. The head nods its head. Why, in your eyes, that dread of not knowing the hour of our coming destruction?

Although Adèle tries hard to catch her head and attach it to her body, and though she relights the Virgin's lamp to plead and promise, and even freshens the scents of benjamin and basil to sweeten her request, the head darts off. Runs away.

Caught up in the breath of the emblem-sign-object, the head rises, falls, bounds, rebounds, hedge-hops, puddle-jumps, watched by the children doggedly throwing dust in one another's eyes. Adèle runs after it, calling and begging, but the jubilant head, curling its lips, enters the darkness of the System and remains there, allowing itself to be touched, weighed, squeezed: the extraordinary, intimate embrace between the executioner and the victim.

In vain Adèle reminds her head of the wonderful memories of Pedro: rain so blue it was misty, parrots from the sky, wedding night in Maïssade between the full moon and the cavalcade of wild mint . . . Her frisky head ferrets around, inquiring here and there: "Neighbor! What happened to Guillermo Sánchez? Neighbor! Who turned the fangs loose? Neighbor! Who unleashed these instincts, these passions, this madness?" The head stops to think, floats, oscillates. Then knocks on doors: "He went to see the others." Weeping, it knocks. "The workers had gathered together, to join forces." Now silent, it knocks.

The doors remain mute.

Pedro Brito falls to his knees in the dust. The dust moans. One can die of disappointment. As from hunger. Failure is a terrible starvation. No one has any guarantees against lost hope. Any insurance against it.

Adèle's head comes to huddle against the crumpled legs of Pedro Alvarez Brito y Molina. For just twenty seconds. Barely time enough to feel all funny, as at the touch of the orange shirt of coarse linen — a light deep in the thighs. Pivoting, the head returns to knocking on doors: "Neighbor! Hey, neighbor!"

Elías Piña cloisters itself in Elías Piña.

In the middle of the main street, where Chicha is displaying the body of the *negrita,* the rooster's remains, plus the petrified passengers on the ten rows of seats, Adèle's head grows drowsy. I'm done for. I was cut on the fly, on the sly, on the prowl by Don Pérez Agustín de Cortoba who — with Don Preguntas Feliz by his side, sweating in his tight, rust-red trousers — has been industriously chasing other heads, slicing-dicing with tongue and sword, spitting: "*¡Perejil! ¡Perejil!*" While I was washing your shirt, your work-smell possessed me. It's true that the Madonna lost her eyes, that the rain came back green in its verdigris setting, that Rosita Rochas's dog was underground up to its belly, that the children were terrorizing their sorrows, that the good Father Ramírez was too thin for his cassock, that the village had forgotten the springtime. All that is quite true, even the bells of the white wooden chapel that kept tolling, it seems, in my honor and still are, in fact! As though I were someone important, me, Adèle Brito, condemned along with so many others. But free in the wide blue yonder, beyond my body. "Neighbor! He thought he could wed the dawn. My head set out in his footsteps. *Mi cabeza loca* that mixes up what's happening with the public toilet, the birds, the hours."

—23—

Elías Piña sticks the contorted foundations of its houses up into the sky like the crooked legs of a colossal dead-as-a-doornail centipede. In the white wooden chapel with the puce steeple, clusters of tapers are burning upside-down, melting into huge incandescent blurs. The river and its rocks trot piggy-back over the rickety little iron bridge. The flocks of white pigeons with red feet, so lovingly raised by Madame Preguntas Feliz, sweep inverted through a sky of streets, calling to one another with disorganized cooing. The fountain of pink sandstone shoots its plume toward the ground. On arms lengthened by two machetes, Don Pérez Agustín de Cortoba walks, wobbles, waves, the black short-sleeved shirt literally hanging down over his face. It's as if the village, with its buildings and inhabitants, had fallen over backwards. At least that's how Pedro Alvarez Brito y Molina, curled up in the dust, sees Elías Piña, a perception he rather enjoys for forty or fifty seconds, gazing at tree leaves and branches sprouting directly from the earth, and roots launching into the air. A broad-bottomed woman of any age happening by in the meantime would — understandably — send the Adam's apple of said Brito bobbing up and down like a yo-yo.

Then, visibly embarrassed, getting to his feet in the middle of the dusty road, Pedro looks around for his low-roofed house with its concrete walls.

But it used to be right there! In plain sight, in the yard of beaten earth fenced with candelabra cacti . . . It was there, with its six doors of ash (not yet painted), the red tinplate sign with black letters (Pedro Alvarez Brito y Molina, Union Representative), the three light-blue windows with slatted shutters and long, thin, rippling muslin curtains, the square front veranda paved with stones, the roof of corrugated metal glinting in the sunshine, the narrow yellow wrought-iron gate opening onto the street. Pedro remembers that the house smelled of mint, coffee, with just a hint of laundry soap. He sniffs the air of Elías Piña without catching the scent of his home. It was right there, with his twelve fighting cocks strutting beneath the calabash-tree. You don't kidnap a house, for God's sake! A house with its patron saints, its cross, its aloe, its painted protective Masonic triangle and Star of David! And its two dogs! A German shepherd! Ah, the German shepherd! A bulldog! Ah, the bulldog! Pedigreed! I really have to get moving on this! Of course, other things are afoot in Elías Piña, strange things. The madness of the bells, for instance. Maybe they'd shut up if you could shove them under a cold shower. Or use a straitjacket, in a pinch. Some chloroform, *coño!* But as sure as I'm pinching myself and my name is Pedro Alvarez Brito y Molina, labor organizer, the house *was* there, with the faucet that's never turned off . . . There, where the old tin lantern with its sooty glass hung from the dead trunk of the lemon tree . . .

Standing out in the main street, Pedro can't quite grasp what has happened to him. He staggers. Who struck him on the back of the neck? But — was he struck, or not? He starts. Who spoke in his ear? *Did* anyone speak to him? Some really bizarre goings-on in Elías Piña! The dusty street's news reports, for example. Naturally, all through his hardscrabble life, he's had eerie experiences. During the massacre of the workers of Macorís — when Diego César, the foreman at Simson's Construction Yard, was forced to eat tar — he'd seen smiling, beaming, radiant bosses with their wives, children, sons-in-law, cousins, secretaries, nurses, bodyguards, licking, munching, slurping vanilla, pistachio, praline, coffee, strawberry, chocolate, and jasmine ice cream on the terraces of the grand hotels. Of course he, Pedro Alvarez Brito, proletarian leader, had screamed and hollered, accused, denounced, cursed, reviled. But the state radio had drowned out his voice, blaring martial music in all directions. Hadn't he been at Mont-Organisé when the quartermaster sergeant Estilus Jean-Charles, enraged by the workmanship on some gilded mahogany and yellow pine, gouged out the right eye of the young cabinetmaker Alcide Edouard? The first time Adèle had smiled at him, thousands of green birds had swooped out of the sky. Speaking of which, who can blame gravity for the suicide of birds? Pedro knows that one should never jeer at saints or angels, or else they cut your virility in two, toss you to the foot of your bed, strangle you in your sleep. Actually, Pedro admits to being a man who respects the *loas, mystères,*[24] signs, voices, shadows. He never fails to make a pilgrimage every year on January 25 to Higüey, to offer white sugar and ripe figs to *la Santa Santísima,* both virgin and mother. And since he knows that he's native-born to the whole island, each July 16 he lights a candle in Saut-d'Eau, in Haiti, in devotion to the Miraculous Virgin. Sometimes he even continues on to Plaine du Nord for the feast of Saint James the Elder or to Limonade for Saint Anne's Day. It was at Plaine du Nord that I saw the Saint James Basin, a muddy pond. The pounding of the drum grew tangled in its depths, as if the drummer were struggling to control its beat. Pilgrims threw in lighted candles, bottles of liquor, pastries, perfume, china dolls, money. Those possessed by Ogou Feray slithered around in the mud, transfigured! I wound up in there too, somehow, my head floating, detached from my body. I knew ecstasy. Then I was on dry land again, covered with mud, as if the saint himself had molded me from that clay. But in all my years as Pedro Alvarez Brito y Molina, a knock-about adventurer if ever there was one, I have never seen a house vanish into thin air with its bougainvilleas, cupboards, chests, sideboards, dressers, beds, chairs, tables, and its six doors of ash — two in front, two in back, one on each side, standing wide open.

Pedro rubs his eyes. A vague something lies at the bottom of his heart. A warning? A presentiment? A feeling of alarm? Just what is this feeling? What sorcery is toying with him? *¡Bueno!* He knows that the Guardia have made the machetes sing over close to three hundred and sixty kilometers of the border for more than forty-eight hours; that some children who survived the massacre will never be children again; that elderly people have gone alive into death; that young women have pissed milk for two days straight. He's even heard that during this time, Port-au-Prince danced at the National Palace, Champs-de-Mars, Place des Héros. *¡Bueno!* But what has happened to him, Pedro Alvarez Brito y Molina, *el mulato dominicano?* And why these troubling disturbances, like the enthroned bird-kite-raptor-symbol-street-sign? *¿Que eso?* What's going on?

Startled by a junkyard clatter, Pedro whips around: Chicha, orange and green, spits, steams, quivers, her hood pointed straight at the Haitian border that runs along a not-too-distant horizon, somewhere behind a clump of *mombin-bâtard* trees that almost always rings with the racket of a whole crew of guinea fowl. Ah! Chicha! Still here, *la viejita.*

All at once, streaming from the earth, the air, the trees, the church, the roofs, the fields, holes, halls, wells, and walls, a multitude — men, women, children, peach, auburn, black, cocoa, shouting, weeping, bleating, gesticulating — pours into the *guagua,* clambering pell-mell onto the seats, belly-flopping flat on the floor, clinging to the outside, climbing onto the luggage rack, piling up there, with burned eyes, cooked lips, chattering teeth.

A little old dust-colored bald man, a clumsy beggar, his contorted body twisted and turned, lost in a large nigger-brown jacket, perches astride the stiff legs sticking out of the window, the legs of the *negrita* struck down the previous evening by the word "*perejil.*"

"She'll be laid to rest in Cerca-Cavajal. That's where she comes from, *la chiquita*."

There's a sharp scent of wet roses.

A copper-colored woman with glossy black hair, her head tilted slightly to the right on a long, slender neck, hugs an old slipper of rough brown cloth, which she keeps touching as she murmurs broken words and phrases. Next to her, the middle-aged man remains frozen in place, his pipe cold, his expression blank, but one senses, deep inside him, either sorrowful contempt or seething revolt.

One could say almost the same thing about Papito Consuelo Pipo y Gonzalez, the driver with the pockmarked face. He stares straight ahead and seems lost in his kilometers. Of asphalt at Santo Domingo. Of macadam at Santiago. Of road metal at Ocoa. And now — of arms, voices, heads, shouts, legs, laments, curses, and sweat on the road to Haiti. But you can feel that the Dominican driver, behind his steering wheel, is raring to go. No one can remain indifferent to slaughter...

Chicha takes off. Chicha whistles. Chicha Calma roars. Behind her a kaleidoscopic tail of brouhaha, dust, and rank sweat swells, expands here, there, everywhere, so quickly and hugely that in a trice the *guagua* has become a tiny bright spot on an immense compact mass, buffeted by the hubbub, rocking on the crowd's breath, on the verge of capsizing. But in reality, it's Chicha who leads the people, as if she were driving her engine through their bodies. Piff! She jumps. Paff! She pitches about. Puff! She makes headway — gas, starter, gear shift, pedal, in skirmishing order. Forward pistons! Let's go, valves!

Pedro Alvarez Brito y Molina's low-roofed house with

concrete walls appears, as if by miracle . . . revealing Adèle, caught in the ample bright orange shirt, in the middle of the yard of beaten earth bordered by candelabra cacti.

"*¡Mujer mía!*" cries Pedro.

The house has just been liberated from the conglomeration of men-women-children (black, brick, pumpkin, beige, peanut) that masked its corrugated metal roof, clung to its walls, concealed its doors of ash, hid its windows, disguised its yucca plant, the twelve fighting cocks, the calabash tree, the faucet that's never turned off, the bougainvilleas, the poppies, the old tin lantern, the dead trunk of the lemon tree, the tiny yellow wrought-iron gate.

All the houses of Elías Piña had been besieged, invaded, encrusted by thousands of people who had come from all directions, so that for a while the village had resembled a gigantic spotted insect, buzzing and wriggling.

Now that the refugees have left, the village shows the sun its unmade bed, the stains of its nightmare.

"*Mujer mía!*" murmurs Pedro.

With infinite care, he approaches his wife.

Adèle tries and tries to recover her head, but her mind skips, slips away. Pedro touches her delicately, as he did when the cult of the System was just getting started.

The young woman pours out her gaze on her husband, from every angle, then attempts a vague dance step, clacks her tongue, smiles, hesitates, squints sideways at his blue overalls for a long study, brushing them, for a moment, with her fingertips . . . and hop! Turns abruptly away from Pedro, pulls the sides of the bright orange shirt tighter over her thighs to cover herself a little, stammers, thinks, then begins to count the candelabras of the cactus fence:

"One, two, three, one, two, three," she repeats in a falsetto. "Three little wind-swept heads. Three little ones hop-scotching," she sings softly, to the melody of a nursery rhyme.

Farther along, en route for Haitian soil, the mass — men, billhooks, picks, women, hatchets, hoes, children, pitchforks, rakes, old folks, spades, axes, scythes, shovels — grows with every meter, lengthens with every step, uprooting bushes, trampling young shoots, wreaking havoc in tilled fields, flattening brushwood, sweeping over hill and dale. Picking up speed.

With Chicha, its chuff-chuff.

During the exodus, two children, a little girl of five in a pale blue dress that barely covers her pink panties, and a little boy of four, almost naked, stop beneath an orange tree. In the dirt, with white pebbles, they create the stippled image of a machete. Life-size. Their gestures — genuflections, signs of the cross, prostrations — seem magnified by their prayers, their reverence, their fervor. They dance. A slow, majestic dance. As at a wedding feast. They will dance for a long time to a profound and inaccessible inner rhythm, as if they were beyond everything happening around them: the bells, the nightmare in the sky, the dusty-street-radio, the heads. Afterward, they will fall asleep.

While they slumber, the orange tree will bear all its fruits.

—24—

Rafael Leónidas Trujillo y Molina will finally understand that the Citadel can never belong to him. To persuade himself otherwise, however, he will call upon the rigor of thought. He will mention the lay of the land, invoke conventions, cite the old treaties of the Spanish sovereigns, refer to rights, exhume decrees, invent meetings on the summit, supply the most lapidary conclusions. He will even attempt transport by levitation, mobilizing the psychic powers of the 2,786 men in his personal guard. Who, after holding endless vigils of arms, will concentrate on detaching the Citadel from Haitian soil. But the fortress will not budge from the top of Bonnet-à-l'évèque, Bishop's-Miter Mountain.

Finally, Trujillo's dream will warp into all kinds of harassment for the Dominican nation.

The dictator will imprison for a certain smile, torture because of tastes and colors, kill for an idle remark, massacre on account of the full moon. In short, he will be bewitched by the tyranny driving him to demand flags and patriotic harmonies from the people.

The master plan will be carried out, of course: Dominican women will be bred with the 20,111 males imported from

Spain, Lebanon, Palestine, Jordan, Germany, and Greece. Thousands of subjects will be born of those couplings. In general, they will be passably light-skinned. But mother nature will have it that some be albino, others rather dark. Trujillo will order that these last be called *indios*. They will nevertheless remain black, since that is what they will really be.

Years later, Dominican women will forget that they are in a controlled experiment. They will fall in love . . . They will create homes, making love as good, saintly, human wives. The intended proliferation of white babies will be ipso facto derailed. Trujillo will be stunned. He will claim that the Haitian border people have cast some sort of melanin spell on the Dominican population. He will resolve to exterminate the Haitian devils. To that end, he will found the *Cabezas Haitianas* Committee, whose executive director in Elías Piña will be Don Agustín de Cortoba. Racism will become the outlet for the Caudillo's phantasm . . .

Trujillo's anger will cut off about fifty thousand Haitian heads; his hatred will deflower five to six thousand little girls; his ferocity will send ten thousand inhabitants of the border villages clean out of their minds.

Ten thousand gone off their heads. Gone with the wind.

—25—

"Two, six, eight."

Adèle stops counting cacti, goldfish, children's hoops, lanterns, to whirl around and around with the voice and gestures of a shrew trying to step over an obstacle: "Hey! Out of my way!"

She sprawls flat on her back.

"*¡Mujer mía!*" Pedro helps her to her feet.

Standing in the yard of his home, Pedro himself feels completely discombobulated. Strange that a man can carry inside himself the sickness of an entire village!

With excruciating slowness, Adèle goes inside the house, to the bedroom. She spits on her chest. And abruptly starts whistling, shouting, bellowing, shrieking, howling. Arms held out like a crossbeam, fists clenched, she struggles, groans, her body shaking.

Suddenly she is calm. Her face glows with sweet serenity, and her voice seems to come from another world: "The gods must not be left to any old mercy," she announces mysteriously.

She draws aside the garnet-red taffeta curtain of the portable shrine. The lamp filled with expensive oil burns cleanly, blue at the base of the yellow flame. The saints are frightened. James the Elder is blinking. George spurs on his horse. Cosmas and Damian change into beetles. Without haste, like a soul at peace, Adèle rips apart the Mater Dolorosa. A blue pottery eye falls at her feet — a fizzing bug, a water droplet, a thunderstone — and rolls, trots, shines, smokes, darts, explodes, overturns the blue-burning flame that now displays shapes and the agility of many tiny hands that clutch the shrine's black satin lining, run along beams, lick planks, flicker from lintels, ignite the roof, climb, shoot up, fall back in showers, jingles, streaks, pennants.

Thinking they see doves, Madame Preguntas Feliz's red-footed white pigeons plunge into the scarlet dovecote and roast, while the bells — out of their heads for more than forty-eight hours now — swing back and forth through the flames, pealing and romping with glee.

Pedro Brito's house burns with its six doors of ash, the cocks, hammock, jugs, the water in the faucet, the air, sky, bougainvilleas, kitchen utensils, coffee grinder, the two dogs, German shepherd and bulldog, and that special smell of mint, coffee, and the fresh scent of clean laundry.

"The gods must not be left to the mercy of strangers," exclaims Adèle, now at the height of hysteria. Pedro seizes her bodily and drags her from the house. She falls, a blue rain between her legs, and gets up again, her arms filled with green birds. She walks, runs, tumbles down, goes head over heels, the orange shirt at her crotch.

Pedro and his wife leap, bound, fly. Behind them, a drum

roll. Don Pérez Agustín launches one last assault. Hey hop! The machete glints and gleams. Hey hop! Hey hop! Music for bashing out brains. Adèle bites her lips. Her eyes glitter wildly. Her voice scampers off.

"He's coming back, Pedro. He's coming back with the birds and the lightning."

"No, Adèle, it's nothing. Just run . . ."

"I see him, I'm telling you, with his frustration, his haughty contempt, his too many legs —"

"Try to calm down, we'll make it."

"I run, I see him, I run, but him, he's zigzagging like crazy. . . He didn't kill me because my madness frightens him."

"It's all in your head, Adèle, don't think about it, run."

"You don't call me Douce Folie anymore, like you used to — you're afraid, too, aren't you, of Douce Folie?"

"Run."

"Wait, Pedro — if I put on a flamingo-pink evening gown, my mental movie might scare him, don't you think?"

"Maybe!"

"God set up an experiment."

"Really?"

"God created Trujillo."

"Run faster, Adèle."

"God's sorry, right, Pedro?"

"*¡Coño!*" thinks Pedro. "Go figure how the mind works! In the middle of her muddle, she seethes with clarity . . ."

"Run, Adèle!"

"It was a chemistry experiment with human test tubes."

"Faster!"

"And mixed results."

"Just don't lose your head."

"With death attributed to moral despair."

"Even faster, Douce Folie!"

Pedro uses his union-leader voice to encourage his wife. It's as if he were speaking in a hurricane of voices . . . in a meeting, at a demonstration, a strike, a march, a rally for fair wages: banners, signs, an endless assembly-line of slogans. And the militant worker's voice penetrates Adèle, drives her on, excites her. Pedro himself, forgetting the maddened bells, the street-radio, the enthroned raptor, remembers his last meeting with the factory workers, recalls their final resolution: "For now, it's important to safeguard love, to keep the connection between the two peoples." The round face of Guillermo Sánchez y Santana, *el jefe,* executed yesterday by the Guardia in the verdigrised dawn of Puerto Plata, appears before him like a beacon.

Pedro pulls Adèle along, runs with her, sweats, pants, until they reach the enormous swarming mass — of men, shovels, rumblings, hoes, sputterings, laundry tubs, shouts, crimsons, mattocks, shattering noises, oxen, dove-grays, women, wheelbarrows, screams, chairs, pitchforks, sea-greens, roars, goats, whirrings, mattresses, ermine-whites, rattlings, poultry, pickaxes, murmurs, oranges, children, cupboards, baskets, yells, donkeys, indigos, grindings, portable stoves, mules, trowels, olive-greens, shears, creakings, cats, browns, old folks, whistles, ash-grays, garden forks, rakes, racket, straw — that surrounds Chicha, foaming and teeming.

Frothing like whitecaps.

"We've made it, *chiquita*. We've joined the others."

"The slashing fires, Pedro? The screaming lightning bolts?"

"That's all over, finished, gone."

"The wind and the crosses invading like a frenzied dictator — "

"Don't be afraid anymore."

"I'm managing, Pedro, I'm settling down, relax, I'm getting better. Don't shout, I'm here. Hold my heart."

"God!" thinks Pedro. "So much gentle sweetness in the floodwaters of that mind!"

"I'm not shouting . . . I love you, Adèle," he says, and his voice trembles.

Adèle becomes a counting virtuoso, tallying up, enumerating everything that meets her eye or stirs her soul: women's hips, green birds, the machetes on display, children's tears, the leaders' orders, the frescoes of the bird-sign, the carnival of faces, the blues of the rain.

She counts Pedro's eyes, recounts them, finds them strangely powerful, so powerful she would have used them for lightning rods to protect herself from the advance of the machetes' thunderbolts. Hey hop! She enters Pedro's eyes while he clasps her to his breast. He feels the troubled heat of this woman who demands his protection. He hugs her, squeezes her, envelops her. And begins to hope that one day, she will recover the light of her mind with the promise of new life stirring in her young body.

Every embrace is warmth and an invitation to bliss.

Chicha appears to lose her footing, seems borne aloft in triumph, yet her engine can be heard grumbling, snorting, scolding, groaning, as if she were pumping a last jolt of energy from the refugees, who — with piercing cries and eyes popping out of their heads — pile over the border. With their furniture, tools, saints, smells, songs, legends, their ways of walking, and talking.

Their way of life.

Chicha blows out all four tires, her bolts, her pistons, her tie-rods, her springs, her headlights, her stories. Gasps smokes cracks stops dead terminus!

The end of the line.

She has honored her contract: to serve the people of the border! Which she has done indeed. Now she can gather up her kilometers. Of asphalt. Mud. Gravel. Dirt. Rubble. Macadam. She will certainly have her museum of marvels: smuggled goods, and kissing couples on her benches, and rural markets, parish feasts, weddings, the short circuits of lightning bugs, cockfights, the enchantment of daisies, festive hoopla, the smells of cities, towns, and villages. *¡Adiós,* Don Papito Consuelo Pipo y Gonzalez! We have traveled a lot of road together, hey, old fox? As for me, my day is done, my time has come.

Staring straight ahead, behind the wheel, the Dominican driver with the pockmarked face does not reply to Chicha's farewell. Angry or deeply moved? Who can tell what goes on in the head of a *borracho* Dominican driver learning to live with loneliness? And soliloquizing?

The middle-aged man lights his pipe. An aroma of bergamot spirals through the air. The rooster slain by the dawn has lost its feathers during the emigration, probably from all the bouncing around. Its naked, waxen body, swollen and flecked with greenish blotches, seems to proclaim that decay will always have the last word.

Left far, far behind: Hey hop! Hey hop! Don Agustín's machete and the long, slender, gadabout legs of Emmanuelle.

–26–

They are of every color, every walk of life, every belief, every character, every kind of memory and beauty, those people who have just landed themselves on Haitian soil. The day after Trujillo's madness, they came by the tens of thousands from every cranny of the Dominican border: Neiba, with its abundant honey; Banica of the four sulfurous springs; Dajabón, where the Massacre River flows; Cercado, where Francisco del Rosario died; and Las Damas, Jimaní, Barahona, San Francisco de Monte Plata. They sought refuge in every corner of the Haitian border: Fond-Verrettes, where the musician trees[25] sing; Perdegales, where the subterranean winds reside; Ouanaminthe, with its aroma of café au lait; Belladère, Fond-Parisien, Dame-Jeanne-Cassée, Aguahidionde.

Are they Haitians? Are they Dominicans?

Together they hoped for good harvests, and trembled in the same cabins when the harsh winds blew. They welcomed the saints and angels with the same offerings, sang the same refrains with the same musical instruments, danced to the same rhythms, cooked the same food, drank the same black coffee, defended freedom with the same turbulence, sowed the seeds of love in the same voluptuous earth. They have so many things in common, share so many similar wounds and joys that trying to distinguish between the two peoples violates their tacit understanding to live as one.

They came to join their lives, one side with the other, with the dream of creating one people from two lands mixed together.

They cannot tell how long they will remain distressed and helpless. But they clearly know that the land they see before their eyes is real enough to bear the weight of trees. And that it is their land.

A breeze brings a heavy scent of leaves, bark, water, which means some old woman is preparing a good-luck bath for a celebration, a deliverance. The refugees look upon the land and take its measure, wishing they could bathe it with the perfume of water, bark, and leaves, to which they would add salt. For strength. And purity. They count the roofs that will spring up: a school for liberty, a hospital for care, unions for labor, a church for love.

And they know they have a world to build.

Pedro and Adèle gaze for a long time at the clear, free sky above the turmoil of the border. With their fingers, they draw, on the dark earth — to be honest, no one knows what it is — a wing, perhaps?

And then, they smile as if they were singing.

A Note on the Translation

A few years ago, while translating into English Lyonel Trouillot's *Street of Lost Footsteps*, a densely allusive novel set in Port-au-Prince, I was doing lots of research and speaking with many people about Haiti. While in a doctor's office one day, I heard a Haitian accent and asked a young medical assistant, Cuschine Laviolette, if she would answer a few questions for me. She graciously suggested that I speak with her husband, who had only recently arrived in the United States from Haiti and would be glad to assist me with my queries.

Obed Laviolette proved a most valuable informant indeed, and I am grateful for the help he gave me, but I am more thankful still that he insisted on generously lending me one of his most precious possessions. Books are expensive in Haiti, and Obed Laviolette had been much distressed at having to abandon the personal library he had accumulated on his modest salary as a schoolteacher. The one book he did manage to bring with him into exile was René Philoctète's *Le Peuple des Terres Mêlées*. This was the book he lent me, and you hold it now in your hands. I was transfixed by this dreamworld of heartless nightmare, illuminated by the most tender and courageous light of love, and I was immediately and forever in awe of the great soul of René Philoctète, a writer of matchless invention and fearless integrity. To my dismay, I discovered that he had recently died, that there were no English translations of his works (which were out of print in French), and that no one even knew who held the rights to *Le Peuple des Terres Mêlées,* because the small Haitian firm that had published it was defunct. After New Directions took an interest in the novel, Alain Philoctète was eventually contacted, and he gave permission for his father's novel to return to life in this English translation, which I would like to dedicate to Obed and Cuschine Laviolette. They are the godparents of what has truly been a labor of love.

The original text of *Le Peuple des Terres Mêlées* contains a few words in Haitian Krèyol (which are either clearly understandable in their context or have been paired with their English equivalents) and quite a bit of Spanish. In this translation, all Spanish words and expressions used by Philoctète have been preserved. (The proofreading of Éditions Henri Deschamps was valiant but not always reliable, and the Spanish of the original text is sometimes inaccurate. These mistakes have been corrected.) Where the Spanish is transparently easy to understand, it appears on its own; when the Spanish is more complex, I have either provided an English translation next to it, or worked the English for a few key Spanish words into the surrounding text. In a few places where English translations of Spanish text would have been obtrusive in the narrative, they have been footnoted.

I have also provided endnotes. The islands of the Caribbean swim in a mighty sea of cultures and histories that are a constant presence, like the sea itself, in the lives of the Caribbean peoples. Philoctète's many references and allusions are like wormholes whisking the reader instantly into other times and places, sometimes into whole universes of glory and grievance, mystery and horror. The endnotes explain the major (and a few minor) blips in the text where the author's Haitian readership would know exactly what is at stake, while the average (or even reasonably well-informed) American reader would be essentially clueless. To cut down on the number of endnotes, I sometimes combined related information regarding different — but not too widely separated — places in the text, which means that although some endnote material might seem a little outside the scope of the original subject, a future reference will soon appear to pick up the slack.

Philoctète's title for his novel, *Le Peuple des Terres Mêlées,* can be translated literally as *The People of the Mixed Lands.* The French title works; the English title does not. The Massacre River marks the boundary that separates the Dominican Republic from Haiti in the north, and the appalling symbolism of its name makes *Massacre River* a more striking title, obviously, but it is not the hopeful and even healing title the author chose, so I think this clarification is in order here. To a French reader, *Terres Mêlées* inevitably echoes the words *sang-mêlé,* "mixed-blood," so that the French title means, in a way, "the mixed-blood people of the mixed lands," which is the whole subject of the novel. The word *mêlé* could not be comfortably translated to retain the original title: "mixed lands," "mingled lands," "jumbled lands" — nothing fit. And yet the word's phantom meaning in French, the sense of two countries joined in two peoples living as one along their shared border, was what gave the original title its deepest import.

Philoctetes, the most famous archer in the Trojan War, inherited the bow and poisoned arrows of his friend Hercules. Wounded by one of these arrows while on his way to Troy, Philoctetes was abandoned by his companions on the coast of Lemnos because of the unbearable stench of his wound. When an oracle declared that Troy could not be taken without the arrows of Hercules, Ulysses and Diomedes went to fetch Philoctetes, whose wound was cured on his arrival at Troy by Aesculapius. Edmund Wilson's book *The Wound and the Bow,* which studied the bond between "genius and disease" in modern writers, is perhaps the best-known reworking of the figure of this ancient Greek hero, whose name was proudly born by Ti René. No son of Haiti ever felt the wounds of his country more truly than René Philoctète, and no one ever bent the bow of his pen with more devastating accuracy to describe what Lyonel Trouillot has called, in homage to this Haitian writer par excellence, "the wound and the dream."

– Linda Coverdale

Endnotes

1. When Christopher Columbus arrived in the New World, Amerindians had been living in the Caribbean for more than a thousand years. Among the earliest settlers there were the Ciboney, but most of the Antilles were later populated by the Taino, who were in turn partially displaced throughout the lesser Antilles by the fierce Caribs. On December 6, 1492, Columbus anchored off the northwest coast of the island of Ayiti ("the land of mountains"), soon to be renamed Hispaniola. The Taino inhabitants, who lived in five chiefdoms ruled by *caciques,* were a peaceful people who welcomed the Spanish with courtesy and generosity, as Columbus himself noted. When the *Santa María* ran aground and sank off the north coast of the island on Christmas Eve, 1492, Columbus salvaged materials from the wreck with the help of the Taino and built a small fort he christened La Navidad (Fort La Nativité), where he left thirty-nine sailors with instructions to trade for gold.

The Spaniards in the fort began to rape native women and viciously abuse the local people. On November 28, 1493, when Columbus returned with the Grand Fleet to the island he called Hispaniola, he found La Navidad had been burned to the ground and all the sailors killed in retaliation for their crimes. Caonabo — Lord of the Golden House, Cacique of the Blue Mountains, the most powerful chief in Ayiti, whose *cacicazgo* included much of the immense Cibao Valley — had punished the invaders, thereby becoming a symbol of resistance to the Spanish. Pretending to make peace, Columbus lured Caonabo into a trap and sent him to Spain in chains to stand trial, but the ship was lost at sea. The cycle of European slaughter and enslavement, which would wipe out almost all the native populations of the Caribbean within a few generations, had begun.

2. Divided between Haiti in the west and the Dominican Republic in the east, Hispaniola is essentially a mountainous island, but it also possesses vast and fertile plains. The largest is the plain of Seybo, or Los Llanos, but perhaps the grandest is the beautiful plain Columbus christened La Vega Real, the Royal Plain, which he encountered while marching to the Cibao in search of gold. During that journey he crossed a turbulent river the Taino called the Yaqui; the name survives today in two major rivers of the Dominican Republic, the Yaque and the Neiba, or South Yaque.

3. In 1915, alarmed at the political and financial instability of Haiti, the United States sent in the Marines, who did not withdraw until 1934. In 1916, similar concerns prompted President Wilson to send the U.S. Marine Corps to the Dominican Republic. During that occupation, which lasted until 1924, the Marine Corps trained and equipped a new national military force, the Guardia Nacional. A young lieutenant named Rafael Trujillo rose rapidly through the ranks and in 1927 received command of the Guardia, which became the Dominican army in 1928. Two years later, General Trujillo used the Guardia to seize power and begin the longest and most brutal regime in Dominican history, a dictatorship that ended only with Trujillo's assassination in 1961.

Trujillo was a crook (he won the 1930 presidential election with more votes than there were eligible voters) and a thief (he amassed vast personal wealth by taking over almost everything: land, businesses, even labor — an estimated 60 percent of the nation's assets and workforce), but he had undeniable administrative and organizational abilities, and he brought economic growth and political stability to a country that had never really known peace and order since the arrival of the Spanish.

The peace and order came with a price: the Dominican Republic became a totalitarian police state, terrorizing its citizens with torture and murder. Trujillo and his sons displayed their *machismo* — a quality much admired in the Dominican Republic — by preying obsessively on girls and women from every level of society. Trujillo, who was rumored to have "black blood" in his ancestry, was also a racist who sympathized with Nazi race ideology and wore face powder to lighten his skin. Dominicans are very proud of their Spanish, which is a clear, almost classical Spanish, and Trujillo promoted the idea that the Dominican Republic reflected the "purest" Spanish traditions in Latin America.

Just as the French and Spanish once fought for possession of Hispaniola, relations between Haiti and the Dominican Republic have never been easy. Dominicans have not forgotten the repeated invasions by Haitian forces, and they now look with some contempt and fear at the misery of their neighbor to the west. Despite the grotesque differences in development between the two nations, each needs the other: the Dominican Republic employs Haitian man-power for work in construction and on the sugar-cane plantations, and finds Haiti a captive market for its exports, while Haiti desperately needs those exports, and must in return "export" some of its unemployed workers. Haitians who toil in Dominican sugar-cane fields are called *braceros,* and in conditions of often appalling squalor, danger, and injustice, they still perform the same brutal work their slave ancestors revolted against centuries ago. Even today, corruption, cruelty, and violence characterize dealings on both sides of the Haitian-Dominican border, and relations between the two countries reflect their bitter mutual wariness.

On October 7, 1937, driven by racism and anger over the "new Haitian invasion" — the growing presence and cultural impact of Haitians in the Dominican workforce, increasing intermarriage between the two peoples, cattle raids and smuggling over the border — Trujillo ordered the army and the local population to kill Haitians in the border region on the Dominican side of the Massacre River. The soldiers were told to use machetes and bayonets rather than guns, so that the operation could be presented as a spontaneous action by outraged *campesinos*. In what was later called *El Corte,* the Harvest, the killers butchered between 15,000 and 30,000 mostly unarmed men, women, and children, many of whom had lived all their lives in the Dominican Republic.

In Haiti, this national trauma is referred to as the *kout kouto,* "the knife blow."

After the bloodbath, negotiations between the Haitian and Dominican governments produced an agreement to make symbolic restitution to the victims of the slaughter; only the first payment was ever made, and President Sténio Vincent kept the money.

4. Merengue and méringue are closely related musical styles that evolved in the Dominican Republic and Haiti, respectively, possibly from beginnings as the pastimes of house slaves who watched seventeenth-century contradanses at the formal balls of their masters and adapted these European dances to African steps. Both merengue and méringue are dance song forms in 2/4 time; the swift rhythm is the most characteristic feature of the genre, and despite modern changes in instrumentation, it remains unmistakable even today, an unsyncopated rhythm with an aggressive beat on the 1. Traditional méringue centers on the guitar, while traditional merengue is dominated by the accordion. Both musics have lively percussion sections, but the méringue, sung in Creole, tends to have a slower, more nostalgic sound.

At the time of its development and into the early twentieth century, merengue was considered vulgar by the Dominican upper classes because of its wild dancing and risqué lyrics. In the early 1930s, however, the rise of Rafael Trujillo brought merengue into the mainstream. The dictator had peasant roots, and he championed this rural music as an expression of Dominican culture, bringing it into urban settings to be performed by large merengue orchestras, although he toned down the form's traditional role as a caustic forum of social commentary, naturally.

5. The Taino believed in a male sky-god and a female earth-goddess who once created the world together, but afterward remained aloof from human activity. Such aspects of daily life as the weather, disease, crops, hunting, fishing, good fortune, and calamity were controlled by many nature gods and ancestral spirits. Each deity could be represented by a zemi, a human or animal figure crafted from stone, shell, or wood, and the bones of venerated ancestors would be wrapped in cloth zemis or stored in zemi baskets. Every village had a zemi house, set aside for the ceremonies performed by caciques and priests to ensure the survival and prosperity of their people.

6. Anacaona, also called *Flor de Oro* (the Golden Flower), was the wife of Caonabo and a celebrated *samba*, a Taino poet-dancer known for her ballads and narrative poems, called *areitos*. After the arrest and disappearance of her husband, she took refuge with her brother, Behechio, the cacique of the province of Jaragua in the southwest peninsula of Ayiti. Allied by marriage, Caonabo and Behechio had controlled most of the island, from east to west, but the Spanish killed Behechio, too, and Anacaona succeeded her brother in Jaragua, where she was much loved. Ill-treated by the conquerors, the Taino fought long and hard against them, but Anacaona finally realized the war was hopeless. Even though she sued for peace for her people, the new governor of Hispaniola, Nicolas de Ovando, felt threatened by the popularity of this Indian queen. Under the pretext of collecting tribute, Ovando went to her village, where he was graciously received and entertained. During a reception feast, the Spanish massacred the Taino noblemen. Ovando burned Anacaona's village and took the queen in shackles to Santo Domingo,

where she was publicly hanged.

This slaughter is known in Caribbean history as the Day of Blood. Anacaona, the queenly poet-dancer, is still venerated as a symbol of European treachery and brutality toward the so-called "savages" who unknowingly welcomed their future executioners to their homelands. Centuries later, when Jean-Jacques Dessalines declared his country's independence from the French under the name of Haiti, he did so in remembrance of that pillaging of the island's Amerindian heritage, and in tribute to the few remaining Taino who had welcomed the first black slaves escaping into the mountains to begin their long struggle for freedom.

7. Henri Christophe proclaimed himself President of Haiti in 1806 and King Henri I in 1811. He was the last Haitian ruler to support an export economy based on a state plantation system of disguised slavery, and for a while he earned enough through his harsh regime to build towns, forts, and palaces for his black monarchy. This colossus met his end in typically dramatic fashion. In 1820, stricken with paralysis, with a peasant army on the march against him, Christophe in full regalia struggled to mount his horse to review his troops. He collapsed. Helped into his throne room, he shot himself — with a silver bullet, as the story goes. He is said to be buried somewhere in the Citadel.

Henri Christophe was a builder on a grand scale. His magnificent palace of Sans Souci is today in ruins, as is the Citadel, perched nearby on the Pic de la Ferrière like a monstrous stone battleship. At the cost of 20,000 lives and years of hideous suffering for the hundreds of thousands of laborers who hauled stone, supplies, and 365 cannons to the top of one of Haiti's highest mountains, this massive fortress with a garrison for 10,000 men and palatial quarters for the king was built with walls up to twenty feet thick to withstand an expected second invasion by Napoleon that never came. Legend says that Christophe once ordered a detachment of soldiers to march over the edge of the parade ground to prove their loyalty.

The literary movement of magic realism was probably born in Haiti in 1943 when the great Cuban writer Alejo Carpentier, while touring the former realm of King Henri I, was struck by the contrast between the New World and the Old. In the preface to his first novel, *El reino de este mundo* (*The Kingdom of this World*, 1949), which deals with the building of the Citadel and the fate of Henri Christophe, Carpentier described *lo real maravilloso americano* as seeing everyday life as if for the first time, a perception of the fantastic element inherent in the natural human realities of time and place that differed radically from the willed and therefore mechanical distortions of European Surrealism. "Furthermore, I thought, the presence and vitality of this marvelous real was not the unique privilege of Haiti but the heritage of all of America," for the nature and culture of Latin America were in themselves, so to speak, both improbable *and* real.

Another way of putting this, as Herbert Gold does in his memoir, *Best Nightmare on Earth*, is that "Haiti's most abundant natural resource is the taxing of belief."

8. On the eve of the French Revolution in 1789, Saint-Domingue, on the island of Hispaniola, was the richest French colony of the age. Then, in 1791, came the most successful slave uprising in history. The many years of ensuing warfare were marked by both appalling ferocity and often astonishing shifts in alliance among the various racial castes and invading European forces. The paramount figure of those years was Toussaint Louverture, who proved a shrewd politician and a brilliant tactician. Toussaint was the ablest of the black and mulatto generals who fought for power, and by 1801 he was in control — of a land in ruins. To support an army to repel the inevitable attack by Napoleon, Toussaint created a centralized, authoritarian state: blacks were

forcibly returned to the plantations, while whites and mulattos were placed in military and governmental posts. The racial caste system was thus re-instituted, partly out of practical necessity, on the very eve of independence, and it bedevils Haiti even today.

In 1795, Spain had officially withdrawn from the war for control of Hispaniola by ceding its colony of Santo Domingo to France. In 1801, fearing invasion from the former Spanish colony, Toussaint led his armies into Santo Domingo, taking the capital in only three weeks and bringing the entire island under his rule. In January 1803 came the French invasion Toussaint had long feared: Napoleon's brother-in-law, General Leclerc, quickly occupied most of the larger towns, including Santo Domingo and Port-au-Prince. The death toll on soldiers and civilians alike was horrific. Abandoned by his black generals Henri Christophe and Jean-Jacques Dessalines, Toussaint was lured into a trap and shipped to France, where he died in solitary confinement in a freezing dungeon on April 7, 1803.

9. General Leclerc's triumph over Toussaint Louverture was short-lived. Learning that Napoleon intended to restore slavery on the island, Christophe, Dessalines, and some mulatto generals who had gone over to Leclerc now deserted the French general and rallied their former allies. Beaten by yellow fever and outfought by the rebels, the French army surrendered, and on January 1, 1804, Dessalines proclaimed the colony the independent republic of Haiti.

Like Toussaint before him, Dessalines made himself governor-general "for life" — a favorite phrase in Haitian politics; in 1805, he had himself crowned emperor, in imitation of Napoleon. Uneducated, illiterate, and a brilliant fighter, Dessalines was absolutely ruthless. Although he wanted a black Haiti, he did not want an independent black peasantry, and he continued Toussaint's attempts to establish an export economy based on forced labor. He was shot to death in an ambush in 1806 while moving to crush an insurrection secretly approved by Christophe, his senior army commander, who then proclaimed himself President of Haiti.

10. After Dessalines was assassinated in 1806, Haiti was torn by civil war between Alexandre Pétion, who became the president of a weak republic in the south, and Christophe, the ruler in the north. Pétion died in 1818 and was succeeded as president-for-life in the south by Jean-Pierre Boyer, who united the two warring states into one republic after the suicide of Christophe in 1820.

Spain had regained control of Santo Domingo in 1809, and in 1821, Dominican revolutionaries declared independence, but seven weeks later the Haitian army under Boyer easily occupied the Spanish part of the island, leaving a trail of blood and destruction. Many white creoles had fled when Toussaint Louverture and Dessalines had held Santo Domingo from 1801 to 1805, and most of the remaining whites left during this second Haitian occupation, which lasted from 1822 to 1844. Their estates were broken up, and Santo Domingo became a rural nation of mostly mixed-race peasants. Boyer deliberately tried to destroy Santo Domingo's Spanish culture and forbade contact with the Roman Catholic Church and Europe. His one signal achievement was the emancipation of Santo Domingo's slaves.

With the break-up of the French plantation system, Haiti as well had become a nation of small subsistence farmers, which ensured that Boyer's government was perennially starved of funds. His administration further weakened by his effort to retain control of Santo Domingo, Boyer was forced to flee the country in 1843.

11. In the seventy-two years after the flight of President Boyer in 1843, as Jan Rogozinski writes in *A Brief History of the Caribbean*, Haiti had twenty-two heads of state, most of them black army officers, and only

one of them served out his term. "Three died in office, one was blown up with his palace, another was hacked apart by a mob. The other fourteen were overthrown by revolutions after a tenure lasting from three months to twelve years." Politics became the province of the army and a small ruling elite as various factions competed for the spoils of office.

In *The Traveler's Tree*, Patrick Leigh Fermor's account of his travels through the Caribbean, his summary of the rule of Faustin Soulouque gives the tenor of those times. The elderly and illiterate head of the presidential guard, Soulouque was elected by the Senate to be a figurehead president, but he took to power with a vengeance. He created a personal army and secret police, used Vodou priests to influence the black peasantry, and in 1848 made himself Emperor Faustin I. "But, except for his tyranny and his executions and the vast nobility that he created — four princes, fifty-nine dukes, ninety-nine counts, two hundred and fifteen barons, and three hundred and forty-six knights, to be exact — the fantastic splendour of his coronation and the showers of medals, crosses, ribbons and stars that he scattered among his subjects, he was a feeble version of Dessalines and Christophe. He ruined the economy of his Empire and [. . .] only avoided the inevitable murder by escape."

12. Here are fruits, flowers, branches and leaves,
And now here is my heart, which beats only for you.
Do not tear it with your two white hands
And may this humble gift find favor in your beautiful eyes.
— Paul Verlaine, from "GREEN," *Romances sans Paroles*

13. The seeds of Vodou, the dominant religion of Haiti, were brought from Africa and grew in a world of slavery. Vodou attempts to cope with the suffering of life through healing, and Vodou priests and priestesses — *houngans* and *mambos,* also called *papalois* and *mamalois*

— function as physicians, diviners, pharmacists, psychologists, and political leaders. In Vodou there is only one God, but there are many spirits, the *loas,* who represent the major forces of the universe and the souls of the illustrious dead. The loas must constantly be courted, placated, and consulted through the Vodou religious service, which is held around the *poto mitan,* the central pillar and axis along which the loas travel to join the ceremony through spirit possession.

14. In February 1936, the Popular Front government came to power in Spain, and on May 10, 1936, the conservative president, Niceto Zamora, was replaced in office by the left-wing Manuel Azaña. Soon afterward Spanish Army officers, including José Sanjurjo, Francisco Franco, Emilio Mola, and Gonzalo de Llano, began plotting to overthrow the Popular Front government. The Spanish Civil War broke out on July 17, 1936.

On July 20, 1936, Sanjurjo was killed when his plane crashed. When General Emilio Mola also died in a plane crash, rumors began to circulate that General Franco was to blame for the deaths of his two co-conspirators, but this has never been proved.

15. Decorated bottles are used to contain potions concocted by *houngans* and *mambos* for the treatment of disease or the acquisition of certain magical powers.

Mombin (Spondias Mombin) is a kind of plum much prized in Haiti, and the *mombin-bâtard (Trichilia Hirta)* is the wild variety, a common Haitian tree whose leaves are believed to drive away evil spirits through purifying powers related to the plant's supposed African origin.

Leah Gordon describes thunderstones in *The Book of Vodou:* "A thunderstone is a flat, oval-shaped stone revered for its magical powers. It is believed that thunderstones were formed during the creation of the universe, when Damballa cast thunderbolts to the ground, smashing the earth and the granite. Sometimes small pieces of mirror are glued onto the stone to increase its potency. The stone is often placed in a bowl of oil to prevent its power from draining away. Particularly strong stones are said to sweat, whistle, and even talk . . . It is certain that some thunderstones are actually pieces of stone spearhead used by the indigenous Taino Indians of Haiti. The Taino deified the stones and passed them on to escaped African slaves when the two communities lived together in the hills of Haiti during the sixteenth century."

On page 21 of this novel, such a stone "has returned to the sky" to signal that the time is now out of joint.

16. Trujillo took power during a time of crisis: in 1930 Hurricane Zenón devastated Santo Domingo, leaving thousands dead and many more thousands homeless. Trujillo gained extraordinary powers to deal with the emergency — and kept them until his death. To glorify himself, he changed the name of the rebuilt capital to Ciudad Trujillo, but after his assassination in 1961, the capital regained its original name, chosen by Bartholomew Columbus in 1496.

17. Juan Pablo Duarte, the father of Dominican independence, entered Santo Domingo in triumph in 1844, but he was soon exiled, and the new nation entered what historians call the "era of the dual caudillos." For the next forty-five years, Pedro Santana and Buenaventura Báez traded the presidency back and forth or ruled through puppet presidents. Both dictators feared a third occupation by Haiti (which tried unsuccessfully to invade in 1849) and wished to acquire a foreign protector, approaching England, France, Spain, and the United States in turn to offer an alliance. In 1861, with the country bankrupt, Santana arranged for Spain to reclaim its former colony, but on August 16, 1863, a small band of Dominicans crossed the border from Haiti into Dominican territory and raised the Dominican flag at Capotillo, signaling the beginning of a new war for independence. After two years of

bloody guerrilla conflict, Spain was glad to withdraw her troops in 1865 and leave behind a second Dominican Republic.

Now Báez sought protection from the United States, and initiated one of the more celebrated fiascoes of Ulysses S. Grant's presidency. The U.S. was interested in acquiring a Caribbean naval base, and the Dominican government was financially strapped, so in 1869 the Dominican dictator signed two treaties with President Grant: one for the cession of the bay of Samaná (the best natural port in the Caribbean), and the other for the annexation of the Dominican Republic to the United States. The U.S. Senate failed to ratify by one vote.

After a period of civil unrest, the dictator Ulises Heureaux emerged to dominate the country from 1882 to 1899. Heureaux, a dark-skinned Haitian, was a cruel and corrupt dictator, but he vigorously pursued economic modernization, and the comparative calm of his regime encouraged American and European investment. To achieve his ends, Heureaux was forced to float disadvantageous bank loans and lease both the Samaná Peninsula and its bay to foreign interests. (He tried to lease the bay to the U.S. Navy, which opted instead for Guantanamo Bay in Cuba.) Heureaux's assassination in 1899 left the country in political turmoil, and owing enormous debts to overseas companies. In 1905 the United States began to administer the Dominican Republic's customs agency in order to pay off some of the country's debts. In 1906 Ramón Cáceres — the assassin of Heureaux — became president and began to put his country's finances in order, but when he was himself assassinated in 1911, civil war broke out, the republic fell deeper into debt, and the stage was set for the American occupation of 1916 and the rise to power of Rafael Trujillo.

18. Carnival takes place just before Lent, and the *rara* festival is held during the forty days from Ash Wednesday to Easter Eve, peaking in Holy Week when the yearly calendar of Vodou ceremonies is quiet. The *rara*

bands roam country roads and city streets, challenging other bands to sometimes rowdy musical battle to establish right of way. At the head of the bands, leaders crack sisal whips at passersby and demand money, while their followers play drums and blow noisy bamboo trumpets called *vaksins* that make a sound like the lowing of cows. Along with the usual masks, costumes, and giant papier-mâché heads, special attractions may be featured, such as the dexterous juggling of metal rods, or the burning of scapegoat scarecrows.

19. A number of Caribbean islands have volcanoes called La Soufrière, the French word for a solfatara: a volcanic fissure or vent that emits vapors, especially sulfurous gases. On May 7, 1902, La Soufrière on the island of St. Vincent killed 1,600 people only hours before the most infamous eruption in Caribbean history and the third most deadly in historic time: the eruption of Mont Pelée on May 8, in Martinique. Glowing avalanches of hot ash raced at speeds estimated at 150 kilometers an hour through the city of St. Pierre, claiming more than 30,000 victims within two minutes.

20. The *mapou*, or *Ceiba pentandra*, also called the silk cotton or kapok tree, is among the largest and shadiest trees on Hispaniola, and it is the most holy of all trees to followers of Vodou. The *mapou* is sacred to the first loa greeted in the rituals of Vodou, Papa Legba, the divine gatekeeper and loa of the crossroads. The crossroads are a central image in Vodou, the intersection between the worlds of earth and spirit, humanity and divinity, life and death. In his magisterial study, *Voodoo in Haiti*, Alfred Métraux noted that "The souls of the big *mapous* wander along roads at night, and their monstrous forms strike terror into the hearts of travelers."

In the early 1940s, during its "anti-superstition" campaign, the Roman Catholic Church began a determined but fruitless war to stamp out Vodou by destroying its ritual objects, temples, and even the *mapous,* which were chopped down all over Haiti.

21. Vodou baths may be given in *hounfors* (temples), by springs or rivers, or wherever the spirit moves. Depending on the results desired, various ingredients are mixed with water, and different loas are invoked; then the *houngan* or *mambo* possessed by the relevant spirit rubs the potion over the person's body or the object in question so that the spirits may enjoy the aroma. If personal charm is the goal, for example, Dambala and Ayida Wèdo are invoked; Erzulie Freda brings luck; Papa Legba combats misfortune. Typical ingredients include orgeat syrup, jasmine flowers, champagne, holy water, cow's milk, spices, tea leaves, *clairin,* vine leaves, *roroli* (sesame), and Florida water, a generic name for an herbal, lightly scented clear eau de toilette. At the end of the bath, a coin is tossed into the basin to thank the water loa.

22. When an assembly met to choose Haiti's new leader after the assassination of Dessalines, his self-appointed successor, Henri Christophe, did not bother to attend. Alexandre Pétion's supporters drew up a new constitution and made their candidate the leader of the national assembly. When Christophe came south with his troops, he was driven back by Pétion's army. Haiti was thus divided into two warring states between 1807 and 1820, with King Henri in the north and Pétion's republic in the south. Pétion is remembered with affection because he broke up estates and distributed land to peasants for subsistence farming, but of course agricultural and governmental revenues plummeted. Pétion died in 1818 and was succeeded as president-for-life by Jean-Pierre Boyer, under whom the republic became a reunited Haiti at the death of Christophe in 1820.

23. Haiti became an independent nation in 1804, but Santo Domingo, its neighbor to the east on the island of Hispaniola, remained under the rule of France until 1809, when the colony returned to the control of Spain. Under the leadership of José Nuñez de Cáceres, the colonial treasurer, the colonists of Santo Domingo declared what came to be known as the "Ephemeral Independence" of 1821, which lasted only seven weeks: the Haitian army under Jean-Pierre Boyer invaded the colony and occupied it for twenty-two years. In the 1830s Juan Pablo Duarte began the movement that culminated in the largely bloodless revolt of 1844, when Santo Domingo declared independence once again, this time permanently, as the Dominican Republic.

24. "*Les mystères*" usually means the loas, although it can refer to the rituals of Vodou. Most loas have become identified with specific Catholic saints, originally as a form of camouflage in the days of slavery (this was called "hiding behind Mary's skirts"); the father figure Damballa, the snake loa, is worshipped in the guise of Saint Patrick, for example, and Saints Cosmas and Damian, who turn up in Adèle's shrine, represent the Marassa, the sacred twins of the Vodou pantheon, the spirits of God's first children, and thus protectors of children and fertility.

On July 16, 1843, when the Virgin Mary appeared in a palm grove near the village of Ville-Bonheur in the mountainous heart of Haiti, the Roman Catholic Church saw a chance to challenge the prestige of nearby Saut d'Eau, a Vodou pilgrimage site, where the La Tombe River sends three cascades plunging a hundred feet in a stunning waterfall misted with tiny rainbows. Saut d'Eau is sacred to the oldest loas in Haiti, the creation spirits Damballa and his wife Ayida Wèdo, "the serpent and the rainbow," who dwell in springs and pools. The church soon realized, however, that for *vodouissants*, the Virgin — who reappeared on July 16, 1881 — was actually Erzulie Freda, the spirit of love and a concubine of Damballa, so when Our Lady returned during the first American occupation, a local priest asked the Marines to help suppress her worship. Shots fired into the vision simply moved it from palm to palm until the priest had the entire grove cut down. The vision then changed into a dove that disappeared into the iridescent mist of Saut d'Eau, where on July 16 each year, devotees celebrate the festival of Vyèj Mirak (the Miraculous Virgin) by bathing in the sacred waters during Haiti's most popular pilgrimage.

Nine days later, on July 25, the feast day of Saint James the Elder brings pilgrims to Plaine du Nord, a village about 60 miles north of Saut d'Eau. Because old lithographs represent this saint on horseback brandishing a sword, he has been assimilated with Ogou Feray, an African god of war and one of Erzulie Freda's lovers. The Trou Sen Jak, or Saint James Basin, is a local mud pond where pilgrims ritually immerse themselves, leave offerings, and make animal sacrifices.

25. In his 1956 speech on *Le Réalisme merveilleux des Haïtiens* (The Marvelous Realism of the Haitian People), presented in Paris at the First Congress of Black Writers and Artists, the Haitian writer Jacques Stéphen Alexis described Haitian literature as the embodiment of the same values espoused by the peoples of the Caribbean, Latin America, and the Third World, but with that distinctive Haitian twist already noted by Carpentier in his theory of *lo real maravilloso*: a "marvelous realism" rooted in the history of Haitian society.

In his novel *Les Arbres musiciens* (*The Musician Trees*, 1957), Alexis studies a family caught up in the turmoil of the anti-superstition campaign waged in the early 1940s by the Roman Catholic Church. Many Vodou temples, which had been centers of resistance to authority ever since the victorious slave revolt of 1904, were torn down, and treasured ritual objects representing the ancestral faith of the Haitian people were tossed into bonfires. This campaign began with a *déchoukaj*, an "uprooting": the felling of the sacred trees of Vodou. Alexis depicts the forests of the countryside as great pipe-organs of musical voices, and his ancient trees speak to one another with the wisdom of giants plunging their roots into the depths of their native soil. Their complete destruction, and that of the time-honored traditions they represent, would leave the peasants literally rootless, adrift in their age-old poverty without the spiritual resources necessary for survival.

In 1961, Jacques Stéphen Alexis tried to return to Haiti from abroad to organize resistance to François Duvalier, but he was arrested upon his arrival, tortured, and murdered. His body was never found.